A BULLY ROMANCE NOVELLA

ELOUISE TYNAN

ARDENTLY ROMANCE

This is a work of fiction. All the characters, organisations, and events portrayed in the novel are either productions of the author's imagination or are used fictitiously.

Edited: Mel from Write On Editorial @writeoneditorial

Cover design: Quirah at Temptation Creations

Published by Ardently Romance

Ebook: 978-0-6453768-6-9

Paperback: 978-0-6453768-7-6

Chapter One

DAPHNE

My back hit the wall of the pool house, Cain's mouth descending on mine in a fevered, desperate kiss that set fire to every inch of me.

I gripped his shirt collar, pulling him roughly against me.

Our hands roamed, his disappearing under my dress to cup my ass, mine threading through his short brown hair and tugging hard, making him groan against my mouth.

"There's no way you like it rough when you're with my brother," he said, pulling away, eyes narrowed.

I bit my bottom lip, my chest heaving, and shook my head.

His expression darkened and his hard body collided with mine, teeth biting my neck.

"The perfect little princess with Kyle," he said against my throat. "The kinky brat with me."

I shoved at his chest but it barely registered, a wicked grin spreading across his face.

"So, you do like it rough."

I rolled my eyes. "Enough with the commentary."

He smirked before our mouths fused again, heat searing through me. He had me pressed against the wall so hard I was in danger of melding with it, but I wasn't going to tell him to stop. I wanted him. Had wanted him for as long as I could remember and I was finally having him.

But only behind closed doors.

In the real world, the cocky former captain of our high school's basketball team liked to pretend he hated me.

Just like I pretended I wanted his brother more.

That was until moments like this—hidden in the shadows at a party to celebrate the latest successful joint business venture between our families—with our mouths fused and Cain's hand up my skirt.

That same hand moved to the front of my dress, fingers slipping into my white lace panties, but I gripped his wrist to stop him.

"I have to go," I said, pushing him off me and re-adjusting my dress.

He scowled as I headed for the door. "What the fuck?"

"I have to get back to the party."

"To do what? Go find your cheating weasel of a boyfriend?"

I crossed my arms over my chest. "He's your brother, Cain. You shouldn't talk about him like that."

Even if what he said was true. Kyle had cheated on me last year, but my parents had forced me to stay with him anyway.

Cain stalked towards me, closing the space between us.

"My brother is a joke. You know you don't want him or you wouldn't be in here with me."

His hand closed around my hip, guiding me towards him.

"I can show you a good time right here, and you know it."

He leaned down, mouth seeking mine again and I wanted to kiss him so badly. Only I couldn't. I couldn't let him win this power game he loved to play or it would ruin everything.

If Cain ever found out how much I wanted him—how much I wanted *more* with him—our hook-ups would be over faster than I could say "dirty little secret". Cain only wanted me because he couldn't have me. I was his secret addiction. And the fastest way to one-up his brother.

In public, he all but ignored me. And if he bothered to look my way, it was to deliver some cutting remark about what a good little girl I was for always obeying my parents or what a total bore I'd become. Which was why I always made sure to pull away first during our secret hook-ups. To leave him wanting more of what he shouldn't even have. I knew it drove him crazy, which is exactly why I did it. I had to stay one step ahead in this little game of secrets and lust or I'd lose the only boy I'd ever truly cared about.

I pressed my fingertips to his lips, stopping his mouth before it could meet mine.

"You're right. I know all about the good time you'll show me. I'll slide off my thong so you can fuck me against the wall and the moment we're done, you'll go back to the party and pretend I'm nothing to you. Or better yet, you'll go back to college and forget I even exist."

Cain's heated gaze roamed my body, his hand sliding

from my hip to my ass. "What did you say? All I heard was thong and now I need to see it."

His hand slid under the hem of my dress again, but I pushed from his grasp, knowing how monumentally pissed my rejection would make him.

"I don't feel like being fucked and then fucked over," I said over my shoulder as I reached the door.

He tipped his head back and groaned at the ceiling. "Fuck Daphne, come on."

"Have a good night, Cain."

I pulled the door shut behind me, fighting a smile. The sudden music and chatter of the party overwhelmed me after the quiet of the pool house.

It had been three weeks since Cain had been home from college for the weekend and we'd last hooked up. And I'd hated myself every second that I'd spent thinking about him while he was gone. My stomach had knotted every time I'd passed his former basketball teammates in the halls at school or I was over at the Cashman house with Kyle. Even when Cain was home, he usually acted as though I barely existed and hooked up with every girl who so much as breathed near him, while I pretended I didn't care.

Yet we inevitably found our way back together.

Always in places like the pool house or his car or a bathroom, which had happened at the annual Corona Del Mar Tennis Club casino night fundraiser two months ago.

I wasn't about to strip down for him now because he was half drunk, horny, and none of his usual basketball bunnies were interesting enough.

I'd never imagined growing up with the Cashman brothers that I'd one day find myself caught between them

—Kyle as my boyfriend and secretly hooking up with Cain whenever he deigned to look my way.

But if it were my choice, Kyle and I would have broken up a long time ago.

Only... I didn't get a say in who I dated. Didn't get a say in much of my own life thanks to my parents. The Cashman and Montaigne families—and our money—were too deeply entwined for me to jeopardise any kind of relationship with the Cashmans. Both sets of parents saw Kyle and I being together as another way to solidify their business deals.

What or who I wanted was never a consideration.

"There you are, babe," Kyle said, pushing through the party guests. He slung an arm around my shoulders and dragged me across the pool deck with him. "I've been looking for you. A few of us are hanging out by the hot tub. We're about to do shots."

I screwed up my nose. I hated shots. Hard liquor screwed with my training. Our tennis coach always ripped us a new one when he suspected we'd been out partying, making us run suicides up and down the court until we puked.

Kyle knew that, he just didn't seem to care.

But I slipped back into my role as his doting, docile girlfriend, letting him shepherd me towards a group of kids from school whose parents had been important enough to warrant an invitation to the Montaigne-Cashman celebration of the season.

"Here she is! Thank fuck for that," Pacer—one of Kyle's football buddies—said as we approached, lining up a bunch of shot glasses on a tray and filling them with bourbon. "Kyle wouldn't let the real party start without his ball and chain by his side."

I forced out a wan smile at Pacer's dig. Kyle's teammates had about as much respect for me as I had for them. They saw me as an inconvenience Kyle insisted on parading everywhere with him, and I saw them for what they were — useless jocks who hated women.

I pitied the girls who threw themselves at these boys just because they were footballers. I couldn't imagine they left the bedroom with much more than a few hickeys and a disappointing story. Not that I'd ever voice that. It was my job to keep Kyle happy.

Pulling me down on the bench seat beside him, Kyle thrust a shot at me. "Here, drink this."

I wrinkled my nose. "No, thanks."

"Come on, Daph. It's one shot, don't be such a buzzkill."

Ignoring Kyle, my gaze snagged on Cain making his way through the party, adjusting the collar on his light blue button-down shirt that I'd pulled askew in the pool house.

I swallowed, pressing my thighs together at the memory of his mouth on mine and his hands under my dress.

He was so frustratingly hot, with his caramel-colored hair, golden-hazel eyes and toned, athletic basketball body. It didn't help that when I looked at him, I felt the same hum of affection I always had for the boy who had been my best friend when we were kids and who had watched out for me growing up. For me, that feeling had slowly morphed into something so much more the older we got.

For Cain, not so much.

He didn't mind fucking me in secret, though. Even now, when he'd moved on to college and I was still a high school senior.

When we weren't hooking up, Cain looked at me with narrowed eyes and a cruel twist of his mouth, like the very sight of me riled him.

He claimed a seat at the table across from us, several of his former teammates slapping him a hello. I worked hard to ignore the way Jennifer Rutledge leaned towards him, draping her impressive cleavage over the arm of his chair. Cain and Jennifer had hooked up last year and had been doing it semi-regularly, whenever they were back home in Corona Del Mar.

I only knew they'd been hooking up last year because I'd accidentally walked in on them "studying" in the kitchen one afternoon when the Cashmans had been out. Cain had been sitting at the table with his head thrown back, while Jennifer was on her knees beneath Mrs Cashman's antique dining table. I'd tried to quietly back out of the room, but Cain had seen me, staring straight at me with hooded eyes while Jennifer blew him.

I couldn't understand how my life had ended up this way. Stuck in a relationship I hated, while I watched the boy I really wanted flirt with every girl between here and LA, only speaking to me when it was to groan against my throat while he thrust inside me.

I had no claim to Cain, at least not publicly. But it didn't stop the jealousy that seared through me at the sight of him and Jennifer together.

He sat back at the table now, legs spread wide as if he didn't have a care in the world, his eyes trained directly on me as he listened to whatever Jennifer was whispering in his ear.

"Come on, babe," Kyle said, with more bite than usual. "Don't be such a fucking downer. Take the shot."

An awkward silence fell over the group, the music from the party filling the air, and I wanted to crawl out of my skin at the number of eyes on me.

"I'll take one," Cain said, swiping a shot from the tray

on the low table and leaning back in his seat. "But then, I don't have to get women drunk to get laid like Kyle clearly does."

Chuckles broke out, and I shifted uncomfortably in my seat.

"Maybe I'm wrong, bro," Cain went on. "But having a girlfriend usually means you don't have to try so hard to get your dick wet. Might be time to upgrade if she still makes you work that hard for it."

My jaw clenched as more laughter echoed through the group.

Cain shot me a dark look, daring me to defend myself and knowing full well I wouldn't.

Fuck you, Cain.

I took the shot from Kyle to calm the anger rolling off him. He threw an arm around my neck, pulling me against him a little too roughly. "You wish you could get a girl as hot as mine. Stick to the broke-down basketball bunnies you bone in the backseat of your car."

Jennifer Rutledge scowled at Kyle. Cain just lifted a brow and raised his drink in my direction, making my cheeks flame.

The first time we'd slept together had been in Cain's car.

I knocked back the shot along with everyone else, trying and failing to stop my gag as the liquor burned its way down my throat.

"The princess is choking," Cain said, discarding his glass on the table.

I let out a strangled cough and Kyle patted my chest with the arm still slung around my neck. "Seriously, Daph, you suck at taking shots. It's embarrassing."

He leaned closer, whispering to me loud enough for everybody to hear.

"Don't worry, I'll make it all better when we're alone later. You can choke on my dick instead."

Kyle's teammates howled with laughter, one slapping him on the back, jostling us both.

Screw him. And screw this.

My parents had no idea what they were subjecting me to by forcing me to be with Kyle.

He was always such a predictable asshole in front of his football buddies. Only, he hadn't always been like this. When we'd first started dating, he'd been caring and attentive, the same sweet, gentle boy I'd grown up with. It wasn't until he'd joined the football team last year that he'd become a showboating jock with a monster ego who acted like other people's feelings no longer mattered. Including mine.

If it weren't for my parents, I would have broken up with him a long time ago.

I'd tried it once last year. When my mother had heard I'd ended things—no doubt after speaking to Mrs Cashman—she'd come barreling into my room, sat me down and told me for the good of everyone, including my own future, I had to work it out with Kyle. Clearly his parents had done the same, because he'd turned up at my door two hours later with an enormous bunch of long stem red roses, a white gold tennis bracelet and a groveling apology about how he'd be a better boyfriend if I'd just give him the chance.

I spun the bracelet on my wrist now. It may as well be a leash, keeping me at Kyle's side and forcing me to put up with his increasingly obnoxious bullshit whether I wanted to or not.

It wasn't a total hardship. Kyle was okay when he wasn't being a self-obsessed jerk. Sometimes, when it was just the two of us, he showed moments of the old Kyle and it almost made me feel guilty for screwing his brother behind his back. Then he'd act like he was tonight, and I wanted to dump his sorry ass in front of everyone. But I had to bide my time and pretend my parents pimping me out to protect their business ventures wasn't all kinds of fucked up. Once I made it to college, they wouldn't be close enough to control every aspect of my life anymore.

I'd be free from all of it.

My parents could *never* find out about Cain or I'd be cut off and shipped away faster than I could blink. Any hope of playing tennis for Stanford and joining the pro tour would be wiped out in the swish of a racquet. Or the moan of a name.

But that didn't mean I had to roll over every time Kyle said something that crossed the line. I was still me, and I refused to take any more shit from a Cashman tonight.

I gave Kyle one of my sweetest smiles. "Cute, babe. But we both know yours wouldn't even come close to making me choke."

The group dissolved into laughter, the corner of Cain's mouth lifting in the hint of a smile.

Kyle dropped his arm from my shoulders, shoving me. "No need to be such a raging bitch because you can't take a joke, Daphne."

"You're the one talking about shoving your dick down my throat in front of everyone and I'm the bitch?"

"Look out," Cain drawled. "Someone's discovered her spine."

Utterly fed up with both of them, I got to my feet and edged around the table to escape, giving Cain a firm shove on my way past.

"Don't blame me for your boyfriend's bullshit, sweet-heart. You're the one dating him," he called after me.

I ignored him the same way he so often did me.

"Way to piss off the princess," Cain's voice carried after me. "You better hope she doesn't go bitch about you to Mom and Dad."

Anger burned through me at both of them, as I slipped through the party guests.

I usually had enough sense not to let the stupid things Kyle said or did get to me, mostly because I didn't care about him enough for it to bother me. But tonight, I didn't have it in me to play the role of the devoted doormat.

And Cain was just a jerk. It really was that simple. Any girl stupid enough to get involved with him deserved what she got. Myself included. I was the fool addicted to someone who would never want me for anything more than a quick lay.

It hadn't always been that way, though. Cain had been my closest friend when we were little. But Kyle and I were the same age, which meant our families constantly threw us together. We were in all the same classes in grade school and had most of the same friends. When I was nine and said I wanted to play tennis, Kyle's parents enrolled him, too. When Kyle joined the football team in high school, my parents suggested I take up cheerleading to support him and pad out my college transcript while I was at it. It didn't matter to them that it sometimes clashed with tennis prac-tice or it made my schedule insane. So long as Kyle and I were together.

So, when I'd told my mother I wanted to ask Cain to take me to my seventh-grade graduation dance instead of Kyle, she'd none too subtly ordered me to reconsider.

With pressure like that it was only a matter of time—

and hormones—before something semi-real developed between Kyle and I. Our first kiss had been a game of spin the bottle at a party in eighth grade. After that, whenever we were hanging out with our friends or ended up alone together in Kyle's room, we'd wind up making out. Until eventually, we'd fallen into being a couple for real.

The moment Kyle dragged me downstairs for dinner at his house halfway through freshman year and declared that I was his girlfriend, something had shifted with Cain.

The best friend I'd loved for so long pushed me away without explanation. Hanging out by the pool or playing tennis or basketball together turned into scowling putdowns or pretending I didn't exist. The friendship I thought we'd shared was so far in the past, it was like it had never happened.

It had devastated me. I'd missed him then, and I still missed him now, because the boy he'd become was nothing like the best friend who'd turned his back on me. And his increasingly obnoxious younger brother in no way made up for the loss.

Massaging my temples, I willed away the bourbon-induced headache that was forming behind my eyes. I should have hooked up with Cain in the pool house. At least then I would have gotten off before having to deal with the shit show that was my life.

I made my way to the kitchen, sliding onto a stool at the counter.

"Daphne, my sweet girl, you look like you could use a drink," Mrs Cashman said with a smile while directing the caterers.

I smiled back with a nod and Mrs Cashman went to her enormous fridge to pour a glass of French champagne for herself and a soda for me.

"My boys giving you any trouble tonight?"

"Kyle and Cain? Never."

We always played this game and it was always the same. She teased me about her sons and I pretended they were the angels she believed them to be.

Mrs Cashman smiled, clinking her glass to mine.

Despite the facade I was forced to put up, I loved spending time with Cain and Kyle's mom. She always said I was the daughter she never had and she never acted like her relationship with me was because of the business affairs between our two families. Nothing like my own parents, who made me feel like a commodity to be traded.

I wasted the next two hours helping her and the caterers while nibbling at the plate of canapes that were pushed in front of me. Anything was better than sitting outside while Cain and Kyle went at each other.

When I eventually ventured outside again, the sun had faded, and the party was winding down. The lights strung in all directions over the pool lit up the night, the ocean crashing against the sand just beyond the patio. A handful of party guests still gathered on the terrace, my mother, father and Mr Cashman among them, laughing raucously at what I'm sure was a truly terrible joke.

I bypassed them, heading back to the far end of the pool, where only Cain and one of his former teammates remained, Kyle likely having slunk off to his room to sleep off his inevitable hangover. In the morning he'd be begging me to make him some kind of grease for breakfast before curling up on the sofa, where he'd force us to watch some pathetic shoot-'em-up before falling asleep five minutes in. Our life together was becoming predictably boring. We were like an old married couple, yet we were eighteen not eighty.

13

"Well, if it isn't my mother's favorite child," Cain said as I approached, a bottle of designer beer hanging from his fingertips.

"Drunk again?" I cut back, taking a seat across from him. "What an unexpected occurrence for you."

Jackson laughed. "She's got a point, bro. I don't know how we won a single game as seniors last year. We were permanently wasted. Good to see UCLA has whipped you into shape."

Cain smirked. "Some of us never got out of shape."

He wasn't lying. Images of Cain's incredible body flashed in my mind—the flex of his toned arms as he held me, the hard cut of his shoulders, or the deep rivets of his abs as he thrust into me.

"Hello? Daphne?" Jackson said, waving a hand in front of my face. "Shit, we lost her somewhere."

I blinked. "Sorry, I'm here."

"It's all good, girl. Don't trip out on us now. You only had one shot."

I glanced at Cain, one side of his mouth pulling up in a ghost of a smile, like he knew exactly where my mind had gone.

I was about to reply with some cutting remark about getting lost in a living nightmare when a text lit up my phone on the table.

Kyle: Baby, I need you. Come to bed.

Needed me? Sure. He needed me to get off before he rolled over and snored for the rest of the night. But I was exhausted and this party had been a bust. Sex before falling asleep on Kyle's Rolls Royce of a mattress was better than nothing.

It didn't matter that the boy I really wanted was right here in front of me. What I wanted never mattered.

Besides, Cain was fickle and distant on a good day. If I didn't play the game just the way he liked, he'd lose interest, breaking my heart before he realized he truly owned it. A part of Cain, however small, was better than none at all. Which meant I had to walk away.

"I've got to go."

"Or you could stay." Cain raised his eyebrows ever so slightly, daring me. Teasing me. Tempting me.

I wanted him. Just like I always did. And he was telling me he wanted me too.

If I stayed until everyone was gone, we could pick up where we left off in the pool house.

Jackson glanced between us as we stared at each other, Cain's eyes boring into me. We were being too obvious. If Kyle found out about us, there would be hell to pay. He'd lose it if he even suspected there was something going on and my parents would throw the shit fit to end all shit fits. It was a risk I wasn't willing to take tonight.

Cain read the decision on my face before I voiced it.

"Prince Charming awaits with his tiny dick for you to choke on. Enjoy that, princess."

Jackson chuckled. "You're savage, bro."

I ground my teeth, not bothering to say goodbye, and stalked to the house.

Cain and his butthurt ego.

The pool deck was empty now, save for the caterers clearing away glasses and plates. My parents hadn't even bothered to tell me they were leaving, having just assumed I'd be staying with Kyle because that's what they wanted.

Cutting through the kitchen, I climbed the stairs, slipping into Kyle's room.

"That you, babe?" he said in the dark, his voice groggy.

I murmured my response, unzipping my dress and letting it slide from my shoulders, leaving me in nothing but my white lace panties. I pulled a tank top from a drawer in Kyle's dresser and slipped it over my head, sliding between the sheets. It didn't remotely surprise me to find Kyle already naked.

He rolled over and pulled me to him, his hard cock pressing into my thigh.

"I want you bad, baby. You're going to let me inside you, right?"

If there was one thing I liked about being with Kyle, it was how much he wanted me. I was addicted to the feeling of being desired. Even if it never lasted long.

"Yes." I slipped my hand between his legs, fingers trailing over the hard length of him.

He rolled on top of me, pushing my panties aside and thrusting into me, not bothering with foreplay because sex with Kyle was never about my needs.

But I let him fuck me exactly how he liked anyway.

Because that's what my parents expected of me.

Chapter Two

CAIN

"Fuck!"

I gripped the back of my neck with both hands and stared up at the ceiling.

Daphne was in my brother's bed right now. Not for the first time and definitely not for the last, but it didn't change the fact I wanted to pummel his face in for it.

That smug, self-obsessed little shit probably had his hands all over her, the thought making me fucking rage.

It was bad enough I had to deal with his petty, competitive bullshit every day. I couldn't stand the fact he got her in his bed every night too. He didn't deserve to touch her. He never had.

Daphne was smart and determined and so fucking beautiful—way too good for a waste of space like Kyle.

The only thing Kyle appreciated about her was how hot she was and he took every opportunity to flaunt her like a trophy on his arm. He was obsessed with how they looked together, the way she made him the envy of all his dipshit friends. He only cared about appearances and pleasing mommy and daddy like the good little golden boy, dating the Montaigne princess and following in our father's footsteps to take over the family business.

I paced my father's office, waiting for him as he'd demanded while he waved goodbye to the last of his obnoxious friends. Probably so he could hand down some bullshit decree about whatever it was about my life he didn't like right now.

But I didn't give a shit. All I could think about was Daphne turning her back on me at the party to crawl into my brother's bed.

She was supposed to be mine, and it fucking killed me.

I'd wanted her since I was thirteen. She'd been my best friend, the two of us spending hours on some kind of court —either basketball or tennis—trying to hone our skills and pushing each other to be better. I'd lost count of the number of rallies we'd played or the number of baskets we'd shot together. We'd fantasized about the things we'd buy and the places we'd see when she became a grand slam champion and I was in the NBA. They'd been juvenile dreams and it wasn't like I expected them to come true. But I hadn't expected how hard I'd been falling for her either.

No one knew how I'd felt about her back then. Not even Daphne. My father had been the only one to notice how I'd started to look at her back in middle school, yet the one and only time we'd discussed it, he'd told me to "let Kyle have this one".

Fucking Kyle.

It was always about him. My parents were obsessed with their precious baby who played football because our father had, was going to Harvard because our father had, and was going to study business because our father had. Because of it, Kyle had everything handed to him by our parents, while I was the disappointment who had passed on business school to play basketball at UCLA.

My father strode into the room, taking a seat behind his desk like some school principal on a power trip.

"Your mom wanted me to speak to you about your... extracurricular activities," he said, clearing his throat. "She says you've brought home three different girls when you've been back this month."

I stared back at him. "And?"

He sat forward, elbows on the desk, his steepled fingers under his chin.

"It's not a good look."

I scoffed. "I'm twenty. I'm a fucking college ball player. Girls throw themselves at me and I partake. So what?"

"Not in this house. And not in this family." He leaned back in his chair. "When you're home on weekends for events or when you're on break, you need to stop the man-whore behavior before you embarrass the family. You're not even discreet about it. You were all over Taryn Binghamton at the Kennedy's spit roast three weekends ago."

I couldn't hide my smirk at the memory of Taryn offering herself up to me and Jackson as our own personal spit roast. The girl was wild, and I was more than willing to oblige her. Especially when I knew Daphne was boning my brother every second day.

"You're the one who orders me home for these stupid events so you can talk us up as some perfectly fucked up family. I turn up. You don't get to dictate how I spend my time while I'm here."

My father's face twisted with anger. "Yes, I do. Because I pay your fucking tuition so you can run around on a basketball court instead of laying the foundation for your future with a usable degree. You want that to continue, you keep your mother happy and you do as I ask."

He sighed, pinching the bridge of his nose.

"You're better than this, Cain. You need to get your priorities straight. If you insist on pursuing this inane basketball dream, at least keep your dick in your pants long enough to become successful at it."

I clenched my fists at my sides.

You can't punch your own father.

My father had never understood my desire to play sport over running a company. It's why I'd had no issue distancing myself from my family the minute I made it to UCLA. Only, I couldn't piss off my parents too badly when I still needed them to cough up the cash for college. Which is why I found myself back here every other weekend for some event.

It wasn't all bad, given I got to bury myself inside Daphne whenever I was here. So long as she didn't knock me back like she had tonight.

"Look at Kyle," my father went on. "He's not out bedding every girl that throws herself at him and he's a sports star, too."

"Sports star?" I said with a scoff. "He's not exactly NFL draft material."

Kyle was fast. He was an okay player, but the team sucked. They'd never make it to the play-offs this season. Or any season.

My father pushed to his feet, his face filling with annoyance at my lack of respect for the incredible fatherly wisdom he thought he was bestowing.

"At least your brother has his life in order. He has a career direction, a future mapped out and a girlfriend with wife potential worthy of this family. What are you doing with your life? Other than shooting hoops and sleeping with anything in a skirt?"

My rage spiked, and I didn't know what incensed me more—the fact that he showed such little respect for my success or him marrying Daphne off to Kyle already.

It didn't matter that I'd been recruited to a top tier basketball college or that if I got drafted to the NBA, I'd have the potential to earn millions. The only respectable career path in my father's eyes was the one he'd taken. The same one golden boy Kyle was all too willing to follow.

It had never bothered me watching Kyle have everything handed to him by my parents, because the life Kyle was choosing was one I didn't want any part of.

Until they'd handed him Daphne.

My parents ate up the two of them together, uniting the Cashman and Montaigne empires in the most permanent of ways. If my father found out I was sleeping with her—that I was jeopardizing Kyle's relationship with Daphne—I'd be cut off and disowned, leaving me with no way to pay for college. And if there was one thing I wanted as much as Daphne, it was to get the fuck out of this house for good.

My father got to his feet, leaning over his desk. "Son, I will not tell you again. It's time you get your life in order and keep your girls away from this house. Understood?"

My jaw clenched, and I stared back at him, anger rolling through me.

"Understood."

My father nodded at the door and I didn't need to be told twice, slamming it behind me.

When I got back to my room, I paced the floor, too jacked to sleep.

My parents had no idea what it took to be scouted by a

school like UCLA. They didn't understand what I'd had to sacrifice to make it happen. Maybe if I'd been willing to do things my father's way, I would have had Daphne handed to me instead.

But that was forgetting one crucial thing—that not only had my parents pushed Kyle and Daphne together, but she'd chosen him too. And had chosen him every day since. It was his side she clung to at parties. It was his car she rode to school in every day. It was his bed she slept in every night.

She was his girl, while I was the guy she screwed in secret.

I gripped the edge of the window frame, the timber creaking under my fingers, and I stared out over the pool and the ocean beyond it.

I pushed her away with every snide comment or bitter jab because it was easier to pretend I felt nothing and act like an asshole than to sit around pining for a girl who would never be mine.

I'd never planned on sleeping with her. I'd thought about it more times than I could count while I jerked it to images of her warm mouth and soft body. But I'd been prepared to bide my time until college and bail, leaving Daphne and my brother to spend the rest of their miserable lives together.

Then she'd drunkenly kissed me at a beach party and everything had changed.

I should have held back. I knew hooking up with her would cause problems for both of us. But I couldn't push her away. Not when she was offering herself to me—falling into my lap while Kyle was finally out of the way.

I'd thought it was just one taste of the girl I'd been in

love with since I could crack wood. Only once wasn't enough and neither of us could fucking stop.

The memory of her wrapped around me and her mouth on mine had me groaning in frustration.

Fuck, I wanted her. I wanted her so damn much I couldn't think straight.

I'd been pissed when she'd rejected me tonight. The moment I'd seen her walk into the party, her tight athletic body in that even tighter black dress, I'd wanted to hear her moan my name.

But Daphne wasn't mine.

Instead, she was down the hall right now, probably fucking my brother.

And I wanted to kill him for it.

Chapter Three

DAPHNE

I woke with a start, my chest pounding and skin burning with the fading memory of my alcohol-induced dream.

Only it wasn't a dream, it had really happened.

It was the night Cain and I had slept together for the first time.

That life-altering moment that had changed everything.

Kyle had been home in bed with a head cold when I'd gone to the beach bonfire with my friends, one of the rare times I'd decided to drink. I'd downed way too much way too fast, but I couldn't find it in me to care. Without Kyle I was free to act however I wanted for the first time in as long as I could remember and I chased that carefree feeling hard, knowing in the morning I'd be forced back into a life that felt like it belonged to someone else.

Cain had been there with some of his basketball

buddies, his eyes on me for most of the night. After downing more watery keg beer and White Claws than I could handle, my drunk brain was suddenly willing to examine a truth I'd long been trying to hide: my childhood crush on Cain was still as strong as it had ever been.

Only in the years since we were kids, it had morphed into something else, something so much deeper than the affection I'd had for him when we were young. I wanted him so badly I might shatter into a million pieces and scatter all over the beach like sand.

Only... he hated me.

That didn't stop me from seeking him out in some masochist desperation. I found him sitting alone in the sand dunes away from the others, highly likely he'd just finished fooling around with some girl there, but I didn't even care.

I'd expected him to tell me to leave, to throw out some pointed barb about me being a drunk brat who should go home. But when his eyes had connected with mine in the distantly flickering firelight, for a moment I could have sworn I saw my own need reflected back at me.

Before I knew what I was doing, my mouth was on his and his fingers were tangled in my hair in the hottest, most forbidden make-out of my life.

Cain kissed me and for the first time in my pathetic, pre-ordained life, I finally got exactly what I wanted.

So, when he'd pushed to his feet and offered me his hand, I didn't say no. And when I'd taken off my top and straddled him in the front seat of the black Range Rover his parents had given him for his eighteenth birthday, he didn't stop me. And when he'd slid my skirt up my thighs and thrust inside me, I'd gasped and begged for more.

It was a scene I'd replayed in my mind, both asleep and awake, more times than I could count, and I ached to be close to him again.

No petty insults, no games, just that pure, unchecked need.

Careful not to wake a snoring Kyle, I slid from the bed and padded silently across the room to the door, slipping out and closing it quietly behind me.

Checking the hallway, I tiptoed across the landing at the top of the wide double staircase to the other end of the hall and cracked open the door to Cain's room, slipping inside and throwing the lock.

The room was dark, only a sliver of light from outside coming through the heavy curtains. Cain was asleep, his quiet breathing the only sound in the still room.

Pulling back the covers, I slid in beside him and he stirred. "Daphne?"

"It's me."

I bit my lip, waiting. I'd never stayed the night in Cain's bed, never had the courage to not only ask for what I wanted, but to take it. It was a risk being in here with Kyle down the hall and his parents asleep in another part of the house. And there was every chance Cain would tell me to get the hell out.

Instead, he rolled over, throwing an arm around my waist and tugging me against him, his warm body curling around mine. His breathing slowly evened out again, and I closed my eyes, drifting off wrapped up in the warmth of him.

His lips brushed my bare shoulder, his sleep-addled voice filling my ear.

"I knew you'd come back to me, Daph."

I stared into the dark, my heart hammering in my chest.

Cain had just given me something he hadn't since we were kids.

Genuine affection.

Chapter Four

CAIN

I woke to a soft body wrapped around me and my cock like a steel rod in my sweats, my groggy mind clearly playing some kind of sick joke on me.

Refusing to open my eyes and kill whatever fantasy the universe was delivering to me to jerk off to later, I rolled onto my back, Daphne's intoxicating scent invading my senses.

Jesus. Was I really that obsessed with the girl that I was imagining her in my bed?

The mattress dipped beside me, a soft hand closing around my cock, followed by a warm, wet mouth and my eyes shot open.

Daphne leaned over me, wrapped in nothing but a towel, her hair wet and her mostly bare ass in the air, her giant blue eyes staring up at me as her perfect mouth swallowed me down.

"What the fuck..." My dick hit the back of her throat and

my eyes rolled back in my head. "Fuuuuuuck me."

My fist closed around the bedsheet as Daphne's mouth moved up and down my shaft, my orgasm building in a matter of seconds thanks to my raging morning wood.

"Jesus, Daphne, I'm going to unload."

She moved faster, her head bobbing up and down and her tongue sliding over the length of me, making me groan.

I slid my fingers into her hair, tugging hard. She let out a choked cry but didn't stop.

That's my girl.

She knew exactly how I liked it.

My balls tightened, my orgasm building at the base of my spine.

She sucked harder and faster, her tongue rippling around the head of my cock and searing hot pleasure flooded through me.

I exploded without warning, filling her mouth, her throat working as she swallowed, taking it all.

Jesus fucking Christ.

There was nothing hotter than watching her do that.

I stared at the ceiling, my chest heaving, as I waited for feeling to return to my legs. I don't know what I'd done to deserve such a fucking phenomenal start to the day, but whatever it was, I'd do it a thousand times over if it meant I'd wake up to Daphne's mouth on my cock.

I lifted my head. "Get up here and sit on my face like a good girl."

A small smile spread across her face and she dropped the towel, crawling up my body and positioning her perfect pussy over me.

Then I buried my face in her, the swipe of my tongue making her moan.

Chapter Five

DAPHNE

"I'd sell you for a sip of water right now," my teammate Jessie said as we pushed through a side door of the school.

I laughed, bumping into her with my shoulder. "Thanks a lot."

"It's not my fault summer refuses to end and coach had a hard-on for making us sweat today."

I pulled a face, trying not to laugh. Our tennis coach was in his forties, with a thinning hairline and substantial beer belly. I didn't want to think about his hard-on, tennis-induced or otherwise.

We headed for the girls' locker room post practice, making our way past the basketball courts.

"Look out, seniors in short skirts approaching," a voice called up ahead, a group of basketball players coming down the hall.

My heart stilled when I realized Cain and Jackson were

with them. Two players whistled, stopping to admire us as we passed, and Jessie rolled her eyes.

"Wow, ladies," Jackson called with a wink. "Looking good."

"Didn't you graduate already?" Jessie cocked a hand on her hip. She knew it made her legs look phenomenal. "Why are you back here hitting on high school girls?"

She'd had a major crush on Jackson last year. They'd hooked up at a party once and Jessie had been keen for semi-regular repeat performances, but Jackson had moved onto someone else the following weekend. Now she claimed she hated him, but I knew if he wanted a rematch, she'd lift her skirt before he'd even finished asking.

"Gotta come back and inspire the boys to greatness," Jackson said, eyes unashamedly roaming her body.

That might be true. Or it could be the annual gala fundraiser at the country club tomorrow night. The same one Mr Cashman had told Cain he was obligated to attend if he wanted to be able to afford to live at UCLA this month. Jackson's parents had probably done the same, given college basketball season didn't officially kick off for another two months.

Scott, our basketball team's point guard, gestured to his shorts. "I've got some balls you can play with right here if you need the practice, ladies."

I patted my imaginary pockets. "Looks like I left my magnifying glass at home. Maybe next time?"

The other players hooted with laughter, shoving Scott. All except Cain, who stared back at me, his face unreadable.

"You're wasting your time with this one," he said, nodding in my direction. "There's no way the princess knows her way around a set of balls, given she's dating my brother."

The players howled, while Cain smirked, his eyes never leaving me.

I resisted the urge to scowl.

Jessie tugged on my arm, pulling me toward the locker room. Cain certainly hadn't been complaining about my skills with a set of balls when I'd been sucking him off in his bedroom two weekends ago.

We hadn't spoken since then. I'd thought taking care of his morning boner would have gone some way towards thawing Cain's bitterness at my rejection in the pool house at the Cashman party, but clearly his pride had been so deeply wounded it still hadn't recovered. It hadn't stopped him from hooking up with Sheena Carter at Scott's party the next night. I'd been forced to sit in the corner with Kyle and his teammates, watching Cain and Sheena from the corner of my eye as she straddled his lap and they tried to swallow each other's heads. I'd nearly vomited on the spot.

Only, it was the hurt that had flared in my chest that had startled me the most. I couldn't help how much I wanted Cain, and I hated seeing him with someone else. But as long as I was with Kyle, there was nothing I could do about it. Unless my parents had a sudden falling out with the Cashmans and cut all ties, my relationship status with Kyle wasn't about to change.

"Jesus, did the basketball team get hornier over summer break, or is it just me?" Jessie asked, pulling her bag from her locker and slinging it across her body.

I did the same, grabbing my water bottle, popping the lid and taking a long sip.

"They're like dogs in heat. You'd expect it from Kyle and his football meatheads. Usually, the basketball team has a bit more chill."

Shaking her head, Jessie headed for the door. "You

played well today. Text me if you want to meet up for a rally in the morning, otherwise I'll see you Monday in bio."

I waved goodbye, pulling my phone and sweatshirt from my locker and shoving them in my bag. I left the locker room, walking the quiet halls towards the parking lot, when a hand reached out and pulled me into a classroom, my bag fumbling to the floor.

Cain gripped my hips and shoved me against the wall, kissing me roughly.

"Does this mean you're talking to me again?" I asked, between deep, teasing kisses that took my breath away.

I'd never stop wanting his mouth all over me and the idea of doing it with him in a classroom gave me a thrill.

"I would have happily ignored you forever, princess. But this tiny tennis skirt does all kinds of things to me."

His fingers trailed up the outside of my thigh and my hands fell to his lower back, pulling him closer, my hips pressing off the wall to meet his. "Tennis skirts turn you on. Got it."

"*You* in a tennis skirt turns me on," he said, his mouth moving over my throat.

My hand slid around to the front of his basketball shorts and I slipped my fingers beneath the waistband, connecting with his rock-hard length.

"You weren't kidding," I said, tilting my head to give him better access to the sensitive spot behind my ear.

I gripped him in slow, lazy strokes and he rumbled a groan, thumping a fist against the wall above my head.

"I want to fuck you so bad, Daph."

"So, take me," I said, stroking him faster and relishing the way he hardened even more in my hand. "I'm yours."

His mouth stilled at my throat for a beat, then he pulled back, my hand snapping from his waistband.

"Cain, what...."

His golden-hazel eyes blazed. "Get out."

"What?"

"You heard me. Get out."

Frowning to cover the hurt roiling through me, I scooped up my sports bag and did as he asked, slamming the door behind me.

Hot and cold was standard Cain behavior.

But whatever the hell that had been was something else.

Chapter Six

CAIN

I sat up at the back of the steel bleachers, watching my brother and his football buddies choke at another game. It was a home game and they were down by forty-two, not a hope in hell of bringing it back.

I'd been cursing my father the second he'd called to force me home this weekend to attend another pointless event. But making me sit through Kyle's lame ass game was a whole other level.

I couldn't wait for the basketball season to start so I had an excuse to avoid this shitshow. The only good thing about the game were the cheerleaders.

Or one cheerleader.

Daphne wasn't a flyer, but that didn't stop her tumbling around in her short skirt, making me picture all the things I wanted to do to her, given half the chance. She waved her arms, chanting along with her friends, her gaze never straying in my direction and it was pissing me off.

I knew I'd left her thoroughly confused when I'd dragged her into Mr Garcia's Spanish room and slammed her against the wall, only to push her away when things were heating up. I could barely contain my hard-on when she'd come sauntering down the hall in her tennis skirt, sassing Scott about his balls with her smart mouth.

I'd wanted her, so I'd taken her.

But when she'd pressed our bodies together and told me she was mine, I'd snapped.

Because she wasn't mine. And she never fucking would be.

The best I could ever hope for were stolen moments in a fucking Spanish room, while Kyle got to have her whenever he wanted. All of it reminded me why I hated coming home.

I'd made myself feel better by drowning my problems at Jackson's last night, letting Sheena Carter finish what we'd started a few weeks ago by letting her blow me in the backyard. Only I hadn't been able to get Daphne out of my goddamn head, screwing my eyes shut and picturing her mouth wrapped around me instead.

I'd come so hard Sheena had choked.

I'm sure Daphne had heard about it. The basketball bunnies weren't exactly subtle about sharing their hookups. So, it was no surprise she was doing her best to avoid me now.

I narrowed my eyes at her, my jaw clenching.

I'd sell my own brother to have those legs wrapped around my head right now.

"Dude," Jackson said, gaze flicking from me to Daphne. "What the fuck is going on with you and D?"

I scowled. "What the hell are you talking about? She's my brother's girlfriend."

"I know that. Do you?"

"Of course I fucking know that."

"So, then why have you been staring at her legs for the past twenty minutes without so much as a twitch?"

My gaze slid to him, but I didn't answer.

"And why did I witness a moment between the two of you at that lame ass party your parents had? I thought the two of you were going to strip down and fuck on the table right in front of me."

I shifted in my seat. "Jax, you've got a real flare for drama, you know that?"

He snorted. "So, you're telling me there's nothing going on with you and the girl you claim to hate?"

I leaned back, resting my elbows on the bleachers behind me as though this line of questioning didn't have me totally fucking riled.

"It's all in your head, man. There's nothing going on."

Jackson smirked. "Whatever you say, bro."

Chapter Seven

CAIN

"What are you watching?" came a voice from the door.

I didn't need to turn to know who it was. I'd know that voice anywhere. It haunted my dreams and stalked me when I was awake.

Not moving from my place sprawled in my sweatpants on the couch, I rolled my head to the side to look at Daphne as she came into the room. "Clippers game against Texas."

She pressed her hands against the back of the sofa and stared at the screen, looking hot as fuck in her tennis outfit. I wanted to bend her over the back of the couch and flip up her skirt to see what she was hiding underneath. Hopefully, one of those hot little lace thongs she loved so much.

She glanced at me. "Can I sit down?"

"I won't stop you," I said, not taking my eyes off the TV.

She walked around the front of the sofa, coming to sit next to me. Not close enough to feel her body heat, but close enough I could smell her Chanel and vanilla scent.

The Chanel her parents had given her for her eighteenth birthday and the vanilla was her shampoo. I was a lovesick joke for knowing those things about her, but I didn't give a shit. That scent drove me crazy and I wanted to be wrapped up in it right now.

But my parents could walk in any second. We were in the movie room off the entrance hall instead of the living room, but that wouldn't stop my mother from wandering in offering snacks if she felt the sudden urge to be maternal.

Besides, Daphne had made it clear she had no interest in hooking up with me this weekend. She'd disappeared straight after Kyle's football game on Friday night and had avoided me at the gala last night. I'd been hoping for one of our usual situations—I accost her when she's alone or text her to meet me in the bathroom at the other end of the country club so we could go at it like animals in heat.

But all my texts had gone unanswered and Daphne had made sure she was never alone. If that didn't send a clear fucking message...

So I wasn't about to bow at her feet and beg her to let me fuck her. If she wanted this, she could get on her knees.

"How's the hangover today?" she asked. "You were hitting the bar pretty hard last night."

"I'm surprised you noticed," I said, eyes still trained on the TV. "You were doing a bang-up job of avoiding me all night."

I looked her way and her cheeks flushed.

Relishing the reaction, I sat up and pulled my t-shirt over my head, tossing it on the floor. I laid back on the couch dressed in only my black sweatpants, propping my hand behind my head.

Her keen eyes roamed my torso. "What are you doing?"

"Watching TV. What are you doing?"

She fidgeted with the hem of her skirt. "I was supposed to meet Kyle here, but he sent me a text saying he's caught up with his teammates."

My jaw clenched at the mention of my brother. I knew her answer would involve him, but hearing it made me rage.

Fuck him. And fuck her.

"Sounds riveting, such an exciting connection you too have. It's any wonder you crawl into my bed when you get bored."

She let out a long, irritated sigh, but didn't take the bait.

Shame. A good verbal sparring was exactly what I needed right now to blow off some steam. Followed by an intense sex session in my shower. But I'd have to be satisfied doing that with someone else tonight.

She shifted on the sofa, her hand landing between us on the cushion, and I wanted to snatch it up, pull her on top of me and get lost in the taste of her.

Would she let me? Or would she be too worried about my precious brother walking in and finding us?

I stayed put, pretending to take in the game playing out on the screen in front of us.

Fuck, she had me tied up in knots and she didn't even know it.

I had no idea she was coming over today or I would have bailed. It was fucking torture being this close to her and holding back. If I wasn't expecting a special visit right about now, I would have been on the road back to school the minute I woke up. But I'd received an offer too good to pass up, one that would take the edge off this little Daphne problem after her rejection last night.

"You know," Daphne said, her hand inching closer. "I

could text Kyle and tell him I'm going home to study. You and I could hide out in your room for the night."

I stared at her, working hard to keep my expression in check. Usually when we hooked up, it was at events or when Kyle wasn't around. She'd never once offered to bail on him to be with me.

"You'd blow off my brother?"

She shrugged, biting her bottom lip. "You seem tense. Maybe I can help with that."

I wanted to say fuck yes, take her up to my room and bang her senseless. But she'd hid from me at the gala and I wasn't her fucking plaything. That was Kyle's job.

Footsteps sounded in the hallway and a smile spread across my face.

"Don't worry about it, princess." I got to my feet, staring down at her. "It's not your problem tonight."

I reached the door to the movie room just as Laura appeared, wearing the smallest skirt I'd ever laid eyes on.

Sweet Jesus, she looked fucking bang-able. She was a senior with Daphne and captain of the gymnastics team and it showed.

"Hey Cain, I'm so glad you called." Laura's hand trailed up my chest, then she pushed up on her toes and kissed me full out.

I leaned into it, gripping her ass with both hands, tongue diving in and out of her mouth in a kiss that made me desperate for her lips to be on my cock instead.

We broke apart, and Laura glanced into the room.

"Oh my God, Daphne! I didn't see you there. Are you and Kyle hanging out with us?"

I cleared my throat, squeezing Laura's ass and giving it a smack. "No, the little princess was just leaving to go find her boyfriend."

I nodded towards the door as I took in Laura's incredible rack in her tight top.

Daphne's cheeks flushed and she pushed to her feet.

"See you, Laura," she said as she passed. "You two have fun."

I slammed the door behind her, backing Laura towards the couch. I couldn't wait to get her perky tits in my mouth and fuck away the feeling tightening in my chest.

Nobody passed on a hook-up with me. Least of all a brat who was boning my brother.

I'd show Daphne just how little she mattered to me.

And I'd do it between Laura's legs.

Chapter Eight

CAIN

I rang the doorbell at Daphne's place, hoping she was home. Both our parents were away on a trip in Colorado or some shit, and Kyle was at an away game with the football team.

Jackson said Daphne never got off the bus with the other cheerleaders.

There was a chance she was still on the tennis court or out living her life, but I'd put money on her being home, annoyed with me over Laura or Sheena or literally any other girl I'd hooked up with, like she wasn't fucking my brother every night.

She answered the door in a light blue cropped t-shirt and matching pair of tiny shorts, her smooth stomach on display. Her long blonde hair was piled on top of her head and from the way her perfect tits bounced, she wasn't wearing a bra. She looked totally and utterly fuckable and I immediately wanted her on my dick.

Only, she took one look at me and slammed the door.

"Come on, Daph," I called, knocking. "Open the door."

It flew open again.

"What the hell could you possibly want?" Her bright blue eyes shone with anger and I'd be lying if I said it didn't turn me the fuck on.

"Can I come in?"

Her eyes narrowed. "Fuck you, Cain."

She slammed the door again, and I stepped back to avoid getting hit in the face. I waited, knowing her anger would bring her back for round two.

Sure enough, the door opened again and she glared at me.

"Seriously, why the hell would you turn up here after you practically fucked Laura Hoover in front of me?"

I quirked an eyebrow. "I'd hardly call grabbing her ass and kissing her fucking. You're being a little dramatic."

She scowled. "Dramatic? Get off my doorstep, Cain."

She slammed the door again, and this time I was met with silence. I waited for her to come back to abuse me some more, but the door stayed shut.

Shit.

I pounded my fist against it. "Come on, Daph, open up. You know you have no right to be mad."

The door flew open.

"What the hell is that supposed to mean? You're such a selfish piece of shit."

I scoffed. "I'm the selfish piece of shit? You're fucking my brother at the same time you're boning me and you want to get all butthurt that I'm not sitting around pining for you like Kyle would?" Anger flared in my chest and I stepped over the threshold, crowding her space. "Hate to get your panties in a twist, sweetheart, but I'm not Kyle."

She stood her ground, refusing to concede despite me towering over her and I fucking loved it.

"I'm well aware you're not Kyle. Believe me."

"Why? Because you actually come when I fuck you?"

Her face lit with rage. "What the hell is wrong with you? Your ego was hurt because I ignored you after you were a jerk, so you thought you'd strip down with another girl right in front of me? You can add asshole to your list of accomplishments, too."

"And you're a hypocritical drama queen."

Silence hung between us and we stared each other down.

"I hate you," Daphne hissed, then gripped the back of my head and pulled my mouth to hers.

Fuck yes.

I reached down to grip the backs of her thighs, lifting her off her feet and wrapping her legs around my waist, our tongues tangling in a hot, desperate mess.

I moved to the wall, slamming her back against it hard. Way harder than necessary, but I was fucking unhinged by this girl.

"Fuck you," she said, digging her teeth into my shoulder and making me hiss. Her mouth anywhere on me made my dick twitch.

"Don't make promises you won't deliver on, princess."

"I'll fucking deliver," she said, her eyes sparking with heat.

I held her against the wall, my cock thrusting between her open legs and hitting her in just the right spot.

"Oh my God, Cain." Her head fell back against the wall. "Do it again."

Pulling back, I thrust my hips forward, my covered cock

gliding over her clit through her thin shorts. Her desperate, heaving breaths filled the air.

"I've never wanted someone's dick inside me as much as I want yours."

Her words ignited some kind of caveman need inside me and I pushed off the wall, carrying her to the stairs.

"If you don't fuck me right now, I'll cut off your dick and mail it to Laura or Sheena or any of your other bed bunnies," she hissed in my ear, before pulling my lobe into her mouth and biting down.

I let out a long groan and dropped her onto the stairs where we stood, stripping her shorts from her body. I slid a finger between her legs, gliding over her clit and making her gasp.

"I'm not waiting to get my mouth on you," I said, diving between her legs.

I swiped my tongue over her soft center and she moaned, spreading her legs wider, opening up to me. When I closed my lips over her clit and sucked, she bolted upright, her fingers twisting in my hair as she called my name.

I worked my tongue over her, licking and sucking, her moans echoing in the entryway. If Mommy and Daddy could see their little girl now, getting eaten out on the stairs in their McMansion, they'd have a shit fit. The thought of corrupting their perfect princess spurred me on, running my tongue over every inch of her, sucking her clit into my mouth only to tease it with my tongue.

"Fuck, Cain, I'm going to come already," she panted, her fingers gripping my hair so tight it made my scalp ache and my dick harden.

"Give it to me, baby. Come all over my face."

"Oh my God." She arched her back, her hips rocking against my face.

I worshipped her with my mouth, edging her closer until her orgasm exploded against my tongue. I slid a finger inside her right as she went off, and she cried out, her pussy clenching around me. She moaned my name over and over, making my dick turn to steel in my shorts, before her body went limp with exhausted satisfaction.

I propped myself beside her and she gripped my hand, taking my finger into her mouth and sucking it.

"Fuck, that's my good girl," I said, my cock pulsing at the sight.

She was beautiful all the time, but she was so goddamn hot when she looked freshly fucked like this.

"Daphne, I'm going to come all over your tits if I don't get my dick inside you."

She smiled at me in a post-orgasm haze. "Where do you want to fuck me?"

Chapter Nine

DAPHNE

I could barely think straight after the world-shattering orgasm Cain had just delivered with his tongue, so drunk with lust, I could barely remember my own name.

Nobody had ever made me come that hard. There was definitely something to be said about fucking when you're angry.

Cain lifted me from the floor and I wrapped my legs around his waist as he climbed the stairs. "We're going to your room. I want to rail you where he does."

I should probably object, but I didn't care one bit where he wanted to do it, so long as he did.

His hard cock thrust against me through his shorts, and my body ached for it.

"Cain, just fuck me now. I can't wait."

He stalled at the top of the stairs, his eyes hard with need.

"I don't care where. I need you."

His eyes darkened and he slammed me against the wall, pulling down his shorts and slamming his cock inside me without a word. I cried out from the sheer force of the pleasure that rocketed through me.

"Is this what you want?" he demanded, pulling back and slamming into me again.

"Yes!"

We always fucked with protection, but tonight I didn't care. I was on birth control and right now he could do whatever the hell he wanted when it felt this good.

"Fuck!" Cain swore, burying his face in my neck, biting at my skin as he pulled back and thrust into me again, hitting deeper and deeper each time.

We moaned together as he picked up speed until he was thrusting in and out of me fast and rough, both of us panting hard.

"Oh my god, Cain. Don't stop." I rocked my hips against him, my orgasm building in my core. "No one has ever fucked me this good."

"Not even my brother?" he growled, slamming into me so hard I slid up the wall.

I shook my head, wrapping my legs tighter around him, pulling him deeper. "Nobody has ever gone this deep."

He bottomed out, groaning long and loud, then pulled out to slam into me over and over. "Fuck, baby. You feel so damn good."

His mouth met mine, our tongues sweeping in hot, careless fumbling that only heightened my arousal until I was teetering on the edge again.

"*Cain...*"

He tunneled deeper inside me, impaling me to the wall and quickening the pace.

"I'm close," he ground out between panting breaths.

With another hard thrust of his cock, my orgasm swept through me like a firework, exploding hard and fast, and I clung to him, my nails digging into his shoulders.

He groaned, his whole body tightening as he spilled inside me with wicked, rippling pulses.

He dropped his head to my shoulder and we fell quiet, the only sounds our ragged panting as we worked to catch our breath, his cock still buried deep.

He looked up, taking my face in his hands, a fierceness in his hard eyes.

"Daphne?"

"Yeah?"

"I'm fucking addicted to you."

I pulled him tighter against me, trying to ignore the obvious.

That the feeling was definitely, undeniably, infuriatingly mutual.

Chapter Ten

CAIN

I strolled into my father's home office, already mentally tapped from whatever lecture he wanted to hand down.

I'd spent the drive back to Corona Del Mar seething over being summoned from school mid-week for whatever the hell this was. I didn't have time for my father's bullshit when I was trying to make the starting roster and put myself on the fast track to the NBA.

"Take a seat," my father said, more clipped than usual.

The old man was pissed.

"I'll stand."

His hard gaze locked with mine, his jaw clenching.

"What the hell is this about? I don't have time for another one of your lectures that you definitely could have given me over the phone."

My father turned his computer screen towards me.

"Care to tell me what the hell this is?"

Security footage filled the screen from cameras I didn't

know existed and there, in all our naked, writhing glory, were Daphne and I fucking against the hallway wall of her house. There was no way Daphne knew about the cameras either or she would have dragged me into her bedroom to get it on.

I had to stem my raging hard-on at the sight of Daphne with her legs wrapped around me and her head thrown back, face contorted with pleasure as I slammed into her, my bare ass flexing with every thrust.

Fuck me, that sex session had been hot. And watching it now was even hotter.

This footage had to have come from the Montaignes though, which meant my father wasn't the only one who'd seen it. Daphne's parents had too.

"What the fuck is this?" my father snapped, pulling my attention.

"Exactly what it looks like."

There was no point lying. It was all there in full color.

My father sneered. "It looks like you fucking your brother's girlfriend in the goddamn hallway of the Montaigne's house, you smug little shit. What I want to know is, why?"

I shrugged. "She wanted it. I wanted it. So, we fucked."

His face darkened, and he slammed his hand on the keyboard, stalling the footage right as Daphne was about to come.

She was fucking stunning normally, but especially when she was impaled on my cock about to orgasm.

"I've had enough of you and your reckless, selfish bullshit, Cain. You're going to stay the fuck away from Daphne and this house until further notice. Is that clear?"

"Staying away from this house is no problem. But

staying away from Daphne..." I shrugged, a smirk crossing my face. "I can't guarantee she'll stay away from me."

His face filled with pure rage and he picked up his computer, tossing it at the wall. It smashed, leaving a gaping hole in the plaster before hitting the floor.

"You ungrateful little shit. You think this is funny? You're fucking with millions of dollars in business deals because you want to get your fucking dick wet with your brother's girlfriend?"

I opened my mouth to speak, but he cut me off.

"You will stay the fuck away from her or your tuition money is done. No more UCLA, no more basketball and sure as hell no NBA."

My jaw locked and I breathed heavily through my nose to stem my rage. He knew exactly how to threaten me to make it hit.

"Stay away from her, Cain. Do you understand me?"

I stared back at him, my expression purposefully blank.

"Yeah," I drawled, fury burning through me. "I fucking understand you."

I stormed out, slamming the door so hard it ricocheted open again and crashed into the wall.

My mother appeared from the kitchen just as I reached the front door.

"Oh honey, I didn't know you were coming home tonight. Do you want me to make you some food?"

I paused. "No thanks, Mom. But I'm sure Kyle will be happy to take whatever you're dishing out. He usually is."

I stormed down the front steps and was in my car before my mom could follow, speeding down the driveway and onto the street.

I'd just reached the highway, pushing my foot to the

floor and diving in and out of traffic, when my phone pinged with a text from Daphne.

Daphne: Saw your car out front. Kyle's been held up at practice. I'm waiting in your room for you. Let's see if we can top last weekend ;)

I tossed my phone across the car and it hit the passenger door.

"FUCK!"

Of course, this was my fucking life.

Kyle got everything he wanted, while I had to choose between the two things that meant the most to me in this fucking useless world.

It was an impossible choice. One thing I wanted and the other I fucking *needed*.

Only the choice was made for me the second our parents had seen that footage.

Daphne and I were done.

Chapter Eleven

DAPHNE

Seven messages.
Two phone calls.
Four Snaps.
And three Instagram DMs.

That's how many times I'd tried to talk to Cain and that's how many times he'd completely ignored me, every single one going unanswered.

I tried to shove down the hurt seizing my insides, but it was impossible, especially when I could see that the Snaps I'd sent him were opened and the Instagram DMs read.

I'd been walking around like a lovesick fool since our night of mind-blowing sex last weekend. It may have started on the stairs, but we'd later moved to my bedroom, where we'd gone at it for hours, Cain worshipping every inch of my body.

I could still feel his lips on my skin and his hard length buried deep inside me.

I'd crossed the line when I'd sent him that text saying I'd wait for him in his room. I'd offered to blow off Kyle for him once before, and he'd rejected it. I knew better than to be too eager with Cain, to push too hard, to appear too available.

It was the thrill of the chase he loved, the catch more than the kill. And I'd offered myself up to him, ensuring his interest had strayed.

I walked through the door from school, tossing my bag on the floor and heading for the stairs, avoiding even a glance at the spot where Cain had gone down on me, making me come so hard I nearly choked on my own tongue.

Oh my god, I missed him.

How had I screwed this up so badly?

***

It had been seventeen days and still not a word out of Cain.

He hadn't been home once, even for the regatta sponsored by one of the many companies our parents owned. Every year Mr Cashman made sure both his sons were there so he could show them off like prized bulls and prove to everyone what a happy family he had.

I looked forward to the regatta every year, mostly because Cain always looked so painfully hot in his linen shirt, loafers, and sunglasses. Only this year I'd had to suffer through five excruciating hours of Kyle's drunken bullshit before he'd puked on my shoes and passed out in the gardens.

When I'd eventually asked my mother why Cain was a no-show, she'd just waved me away, saying he was busy with college.

Busy with what?

Studying? Basketball? Girls?

What was so goddamn important that he couldn't return my calls or texts?

I downed the rest of my champagne, dumping the empty glass on a nearby table and marching to a secluded spot by the water.

I pulled out my phone and dialed Cain's number. Unsurprisingly, it went to voicemail.

"It's Daphne, but I know you already know that given you're screening my calls. I just wanted to tell you that I'm so fucking disappointed in you. Where the hell do you get off giving me the best fucking orgasms of my life and then disappearing? I've spent the day at this stupid regatta watching your brother getting drunk before he puked all over me and passed out. How dare you leave me here. What the hell is going on, Cain?"

I slumped against the tree, the anger slowly ebbing as the hurt took its place.

"Why do we have to play these games?" I said quietly, tears filling my eyes. "Why do we have to keep hurting each other?"

I sniffed, wiping my nose with the back of my hand.

"I miss you."

Chapter Twelve

CAIN

I listened to Daphne's voicemail for the eighteenth fucking time, my chest splitting open at how defeated she sounded.

I wanted to blame it on my idiot brother and claim that living with him would make anyone feel that way. But this was on me.

She'd tried everything to reach out and I'd ignored her every time.

I wanted to tell her that I didn't have a choice, but there was no fucking way she'd understand. Because I was making a choice. I just wasn't choosing her and I didn't have the balls to look her in the eye or even hear it in her voice when she learned the truth.

I'd always said she deserved better than Kyle, but she deserved better than me too.

She deserved someone who loved her for more than how good she looked on his arm or because Mommy and

Daddy told him too. And she deserved someone who'd choose her, even when it was hard.

That guy wasn't Kyle.

And it definitely wasn't me.

Because I was weak and I'd chosen my dreams and my future over the girl I'd loved for most of my life.

And she deserved better.

Chapter Thirteen

DAPHNE

Sweat was running down my back, my brow, even under my bra, from the intense practice Coach had just put us through.

He blew the whistle, each of us rushing to the sidelines and downing half our water bottles.

"That practice was hell on earth," Jessie said, working to catch her breath.

I nodded, taking another long swig from my bottle. "The worst."

Coach came over, hands on his hips and expression serious. "Daphne, can I have a word?"

I pulled a face at Jessie, following Coach to the other end of the court.

"I wanted to speak with you about your performance."

My eyes widened. "My performance?"

"You've been putting in the work, but it doesn't seem like your heart is in it at the moment."

Because my heart was off somewhere in LA.

Where Cain was likely sleeping with every girl who offered and consciously ignoring my texts.

"I wanted to check in, make sure everything is okay with you."

I forced out a smile. "Everything is fine."

Coach scrutinized me for a moment before he conceded. "Okay, well, if that changes, you let me know. My door is always open."

I nodded, heading for the locker room.

I wasn't about to confide in my coach that the boy I loved didn't love me back. That he'd fucked me and then fucked me over, just like I'd known he would, yet I'd still been foolish enough to get involved with him in the first place.

Tossing my water bottle in my bag, I pulled my phone from my locker and found a text from Kyle.

Kyle: Hey baby, you still coming round to hang out tonight? I miss you.

Missed me? The only thing Kyle missed about me were the holes in my body.

It had been a long day and I couldn't be bothered dealing with him tonight.

Me: Sorry, practice ran late. I'm wiped. Can we hang out tomorrow night?

. . .

By the time I got home, Kyle still hadn't replied. Which most likely meant he was mad at me for not dropping everything when he wanted to see me.

But I couldn't find it in me to care.

I made my way to my room and took a scalding hot shower, letting the water wash away another shitty day. I was thankfully dried and dressed when my mom let herself into my room without knocking, a standard occurrence for her, given she felt entitled to my entire life.

"Sweetheart, how was practice?" she said, hovering by the door.

I picked up the hairbrush from my dresser, brushing the knots from my wet hair. "Tiring, but fine."

My mom tilted her head at me. "I got a message earlier. You were supposed to see Kyle tonight and you cancelled. Is everything okay?"

I blew out a long breath. I'd cancelled on him twenty minutes ago and already my mother knew? This situation was beyond suffocating.

"I'm tired, Mom. I didn't feel like hanging out tonight. I just want to crawl into bed and call it a day."

My mom sighed, sitting on the edge of my bed. "I know you've been down lately, but I have a secret to tell you that I think will make everything better."

Unless the secret was that Cain was at the door, begging for my forgiveness, I wasn't interested. But I had no choice but to humor her.

"Okay...."

She nodded, a grin spreading across her face. "I have insider knowledge that a certain someone went ring shopping last month."

I stilled, the hairbrush slipping from my fingers. "I'm sorry... what?"

"That's right," my mother said with a grin. "Kyle is going to propose to you before winter formal."

My stomach bottomed out and I clutched the dresser for support.

Kyle was going to... *propose*?

Just when I thought my life couldn't get any more fucked up, my mother springs this on me like it will brighten my entire world. There was no way I wanted to spend the rest of my life with Kyle. That had never been in the plan. Surely, he didn't want that either?

"I knew you'd be excited," my mother said, misreading my stunned expression.

"Mom... I'm not... I don't..."

She got to her feet and took my hand. "I know it's a lot to process. Just make sure you act surprised when it happens." She brushed my hair back from my face. "Oh honey, your father and I are so excited for you. You're going to have an amazing future with Kyle. And you're going to love it at Harvard."

"Harvard? Mom, I'm going to Stanford."

She waved a hand at me, chuckling like I was slow. "You can't live on the other side of the country from your fiancé, Daphne. You'll have to transfer to Harvard after freshman year to be with Kyle. The two of you can get a place off-campus together. I've already spoken to Daddy and he and I have agreed to pay for it."

She walked to the door, my chest seizing with panic at every word she'd just uttered.

There was no way I was going to marry Kyle. And even less chance I'd give up my dream of going to Stanford to play tennis.

"Mom, wait... I can't marry Kyle."

She frowned. "Of course you can, sweetie. You love Kyle."

"N-no..." I stumbled over my words. "I don't. I love Cain."

Her expression fell. "Excuse me?"

"I love Cain," I said, biting the inside of my cheek. "I've been in love with him since we were kids."

She shook her head. "Oh honey, that's just a childhood crush. You don't throw your future away for those kinds of feelings."

"It's so much more than that. Cain is the one I want to be with. I can't marry Kyle."

My mother's face tightened. "Honey... marrying Kyle is what's best for this family, which means it's what's best for you. Cain isn't right for you. Kyle loves you."

"Are you not listening? I don't want to marry Kyle!"

She pressed her lips together. "Daphne, listen to me. Life isn't beer and skittles. Sometimes we have to make sacrifices for the good of everyone."

She sighed.

"Marrying Kyle is what's best. So, when he asks, you will accept. Do you hear me? We've spent years cultivating a meaningful relationship between the two of you. Your father and I will not let you ruin it now for some lust-fueled drama with Cain."

Before I could utter another word, she was gone, shutting the door behind her.

But I didn't hesitate. I pulled a duffel bag from under my bed and started piling clothes in. There was no way in hell I was going to let my parents force me into a marriage I didn't want, in a relationship I'd never wanted to be a part of.

I was done being a pawn in their game.

And I was going to finally take exactly what I wanted.

I crept down the hall and into the garage, tossing my duffel bag on the passenger seat. The garage door was already halfway up when I started the engine on the Jeep my parents had bought me for my sweet sixteenth.

It was unlikely they'd even hear me leave, far too engrossed in what had to be a fraught conversation about their wayward daughter and her refusal to marry a boy they'd forced on her when she was too young to know better.

It would take just shy of two hours to drive to my destination, but I had to make a stop first.

I turned into the Cashman's driveway, pulling up beside Kyle's tricked out truck and running up the steps to the front door. I let myself in like I always did, finding Kyle sprawled on his bed, a girl-on-girl porn playing on his laptop and his hand down his shorts.

"Hey baby," he said, eyes hazy with desire. "Thank fuck you're here, you can finish me off instead."

He gestured to his hard-on, and I resisted the urge to roll my eyes.

"Kyle, we need to talk."

"Can we talk later? I really want to come in your mouth."

He sat up, swinging his legs over the side of the bed and motioning for me to get on my knees.

"Kyle, I'm not going to suck your dick right now. Can you read the room? I'm breaking up with you."

His hand snapped from his waistband. "You're what?"

"I'm breaking up with you. I'm not in love with you and I'm not sure I ever was."

He snorted a laugh. "Really, Daph? This shit again? You've pulled this before and it didn't last. We both know

I'll buy you some expensive gift and you'll be riding my dick and moaning my name within the hour."

Anger burned inside me. The only reason that had ever happened is because my parents had made me take him back.

"Think what you want, I'm done," I said, turning to leave.

"Is this about my fucking brother?"

I stilled.

"He doesn't want you, Daphne. He only wants to fuck you. And even then, it's just to piss me off."

My gaze roamed his face for any hint of jealousy. "You knew we were sleeping together?"

Kyle snorted. "Sleeping together? I'd hardly call him fucking you in public bathrooms sleeping together, but if you want to romance it like some desperate simp and pretend it's more than it is, go right ahead."

I clamped down on the hurt searing through me.

"Why do you think he's ignoring your calls? He's done with you, Daph. So if you want to salvage this between us for the sake of our families, you better come over here and get on your knees to apologize."

My stomach twisted and bile clawed up my throat.

"I meant what I said, Kyle... we're done."

***

Two hours later, I found myself outside Cain's door in the off-campus house he shared with his teammates near UCLA.

Kyle's words had played over and over in my mind the entire ride here, filling me with doubt.

How long had he known about me and Cain? And had

he said those things about Cain using me because Cain had said them? Or because Kyle believed it?

Maybe it was both.

I didn't let my creeping doubt stop me from ringing the doorbell. The thought of being forced into marriage with Kyle terrified me and if I was going to stand up to my parents, I needed Cain to help me do it.

A super tall guy with black hair, dark brown eyes and straight white teeth answered the door.

"Can I help you, sweetheart?"

I toyed with the car keys in my hand to cover my nerves. "Is Cain home?"

He motioned for me to come inside and I followed him to a living room where several guys were sprawled on an enormous sectional, Cain included.

His eyes landed on me, registering the briefest hint of surprise before it was replaced with cool disinterest. "What are you doing here, Daphne?"

"Um... can we talk?"

"Uh oh, look out, Cashman. You're in trouble."

I gave his teammate a tight smile. "No, no. It's nothing like that."

"I don't care what it's like," Cain said, not moving from the couch. "You shouldn't be here."

I bit the inside of my cheek at his harsh tone. "Can we please just talk?"

"For fuck's sake." Cain got to his feet, brushing past me and I followed after him, heading for a door to the right at the front of the house. When I entered the room, he slammed it behind me.

"What do you want?"

I frowned, utterly confused. Why was he so angry with

me? What had happened since that hot night we'd spent at my place?

"I want to talk."

He scowled. "Why? Was me ignoring your texts and phone calls not clear enough? You want to keep coming back for more like a kicked puppy?"

Hurt and anger rolled inside me and I was ready to snap. I'd taken it from my mother and Kyle already tonight. I didn't need another person telling me I wasn't good enough. I'd come here for support, because despite all the secrets and the lies and the taunts, all the bullshit we'd put each other through, I loved him. I always had.

And right now, I needed him.

"I don't know why you've been ignoring me. And frankly, I don't even care."

He looked momentarily surprised.

"My mother came to me tonight and told me that Kyle is going to propose before winter formal."

Cain's expression darkened worse than I'd ever seen it, his body vibrating with unchecked anger.

"When she said it, all I could think about was you." I took a step towards him. "I've spent so much of my life doing what I was told and being with Kyle because I was supposed to be, not because I wanted to be."

I reached for Cain, taking his hand.

"I told her I wouldn't marry Kyle. I told her it's you I want to be with."

He stared down at me, his face unreadable.

"And I broke up with Kyle."

Silence hung between us, Cain's eyes bouncing between mine like he couldn't process the words I'd just uttered.

Then his expression shuttered and he took a step back, my hand slipping from his.

"That's a cute story, princess, but I'm not sure why you think I'd care."

My heart stuttered in my chest, my breath catching in my throat.

"You don't... I don't..."

I'd denied my parents, broken up with Kyle, and told Cain he was the one I wanted. And this was his reaction?

"Cain, I want you. I'm choosing you," I said, moving to close the space between us again.

He pulled away, crossing his arms over his chest. "Yeah, well, I'm not choosing you. I don't know how that wasn't clear from my total silence for weeks. I'm not your knight in shining armor who's going to save you from the big, bad relationship with my brother that you willingly signed up for. I don't know why you'd come here."

He moved in close, getting in my face now, his expression twisted with disdain.

"Unless it's for a quick fuck."

Tears stung my eyes and I clenched my jaw, refusing to let them fall. But one defied me, slowly sliding down my cheek.

Cain's eyes tracked it, cementing my humiliation.

"You really are an asshole," I said on a broken, shaky breath. "You're a heartless, spineless asshole, and I don't know why I ever thought I could trust you."

He scoffed. "I'm glad we finally agree on something."

I turned and gripped the door handle, flinging it open and bolting for the front door.

I was out and down the steps in seconds, running from the house and the boy who'd just shattered my heart.

Chapter Fourteen

DAPHNE

My eyes were red raw and my cheeks stained with tears by the time I made it home.

I'd cried just about the entire drive back to Corona Del Mar, my heart breaking as Cain's words replayed in my mind.

'I don't know why you'd come here. Unless it's for a quick fuck.'

What else did I need to hear before I'd accept that's all I'd ever been to him?

I pressed my lips together so hard it hurt, trying to stem the tears that threatened to fall all over again, as I walked through the front door.

"Where the hell have you been?" my mother said, my parents sitting on the stairs waiting for me.

It was almost the exact same spot Cain had fucked me into oblivion the night they'd been away. The thought made me want to laugh through my tears, despite their livid expressions.

"You went to see Cain, didn't you?"

I dropped my keys in the bowl by the door. "Yes."

My father stalked over. "What is wrong with you, Daphne? Why are you throwing away your future for that boy?"

I shook my head. "He's not some boy, Dad. I love him."

He scoffed. "You're eighteen. You don't know what real love is. It isn't some high school infatuation."

I sucked in a deep breath, too strung out from crying half the drive home to feel much of anything. "You don't need to worry about my feelings for Cain. He made it quite clear he doesn't feel the same."

"Well, thank god for that," my father said. "At least one of you has some goddamn sense."

I walked over to the stairs, sitting down and burying my face in my hands.

"You've always been such a smart girl. We don't understand where all this is coming from. You love Kyle, you've been with him for years. Why would you throw it all away when you're so close to getting what you want?"

I lifted my head. "What I want? When have I ever wanted this? Kyle and I being together is what you wanted! It's never been what I wanted."

"Kyle is good for you and good to you," my father said.

"Good to me?" I asked, incredulous. "The boy who forces me to drink and party and have sex with him whenever he wants?"

"You didn't seem to have any problem having sex with Cain in my hallway!" my father boomed.

I reared back, eyes wide. "How do you know that?"

But my father ignored me.

"You betrayed Kyle and you betrayed your family. Which is why we're going over to the Cashman house first thing tomorrow and you're going to beg Kyle for forgiveness and pray he takes you back. Or you can kiss tennis at Stanford goodbye."

I stared between him and my mother, both of them unyielding.

What did it matter anymore? It was over with Cain. He'd never wanted me for more than a hookup. If getting back with Kyle meant I'd get at least one year at Stanford before being forced to transfer to Harvard and live Kyle's dream, then I'd do it.

Because one year of my life being mine was better than nothing at all.

And I had nothing left to lose.

Chapter Fifteen

CAIN

"FUCK!"

I slammed the bar back into the rack so hard the whole thing trembled. Gripping the back of my neck with both hands, I cursed at the ceiling, pacing the empty gym.

It wasn't even five am so it was no surprise I was the only one here. But I hadn't been able to sleep a wink last night. Not after Daphne's unwelcome visit.

Why did she have to come here?

Why did she have to tell me my fucking brother was going to ask her to marry him

And why the hell did she have to tell me she wanted to be with me?

The moment she walked into the room I'd wanted to take her in my arms and kiss the fuck out of her. But that one kiss could have jeopardized my entire future. One taste of her lips and my tuition, my spot on the team, and any chance I had of making the NBA would be gone.

No kiss was worth that... *right?*

But when she'd dropped the bomb about Kyle's proposal, I'd been ready to commit cold-blooded murder. If my brother had been in the room I would have wrapped my hands around his throat and never let go.

He didn't love her or deserve her. He barely even wanted her. He only wanted the praise and attention being with her brought. From our parents, from his friends, even from me.

There was no fucking way Daphne could marry him. I was the one who was in love with her.

And she'd said she wanted me too. Only instead of telling her I felt the same, I'd shamed her for it and pushed her away like the pathetic asshole I was. All because I was a selfish and cared more about saving my own ass.

I leaned my hands on the weight bar, my head hanging in shame.

I'd royally fucked up. Maybe the biggest fuck up of my life.

Because none of this mattered without her and I should have realised it from the start.

None of it was more important than the only girl I'd ever been in love with.

Chapter Sixteen

CAIN

I'd broken just about every road rule in California, doubling the speed limit most of the way as I gunned it back to Corona Del Mar.

I skidded to a stop outside my house, gripping the steering wheel and blowing out several long breaths.

There was no fucking way Kyle was marrying Daphne. I'd sacrifice everything to stop it from happening, starting with telling my family the truth. Then I'd go to Daphne and tell her what a fucking idiot I was. I'd lay it all on the line and beg her to be with me, if that's what it took.

Unlocking the front door, I strolled in, slamming it behind me.

"Mom, I'm home," I called to the only family member I cared about seeing.

My father and brother burst from my father's office, both of them red-faced and livid.

"What the fuck have you done, Cain? I told you to stay the hell away from Daphne."

"I stayed away from her."

"Then you want to tell me why the hell she came here and broke things off with your brother?" my father said, pointing behind him to where Kyle stood.

I glanced at him. "Probably because he's a spineless, vindictive little weasel who never deserved her and Daphne finally realized it."

Kyle started towards me. "I'll kick your teeth in for that..."

Our father stilled him with a hand to the chest.

"I warned you not to interfere in this partnership, Cain. And I told you exactly what would happen if you did."

"And I'm here to tell you I don't give a fuck."

My father's eyes narrowed. "What did you just say?"

"I said I don't care. I want to be with her. If you want to cut me off and take away my future, go right ahead. She's worth it."

My father's jaw clenched, but it was my brother who spoke.

"You're never going to touch her again. It's only a matter of time before she comes back to me and it'll be my name she's moaning for the rest of her life."

My father snapped at Kyle to cut the profanity and I threw my head back and laughed to cover the rage burning through me. If he spoke about Daphne like that again, I'd bury him.

"What makes you think, little brother, you ever really made her do it at all?"

Kyle looked like he wanted to murder me and I relished it, motioning for him to try

"Enough!" my father said.

There was a shuffle outside the front door and the door-bell rang.

My mother emerged from the sunroom. "What's going on?"

Kyle stalked past me, knocking his shoulder into mine, before opening the front door. He stepped aside, Mr and Mrs Montaigne entering, followed by Daphne.

Her eyes were red-rimmed and swollen and my chest tightened at the sight.

I'd been the one to do that to her.

"Daph...." I started towards her, but Mr Montaigne cut me off.

"Don't take another step near my daughter."

I stilled, my eyes cutting from him to Daphne, but she wouldn't look at me.

"We've come to sort this mess out," Mr Montaigne said. "Daphne, is there something you'd like to say to Kyle?"

Kyle crossed his arms like the smug asshole he was.

She glanced at him, but said nothing.

"Don't you dare embarrass me any more than you already have," her father warned.

Daphne stared back at him. The sweet little firecracker I knew was nowhere to be found. Her eyes, usually shining with light, were dull. Lifeless. Defeated.

But then she took a deep breath and stood tall, pushing her shoulders back.

"I'm not getting back together with Kyle. I don't want it." She shook her head. "I'm your daughter. Not some prize for you to pimp out to your friends to sweeten your business deals." She turned to my brother. "I don't love you. And you don't love me. I'm done playing this game."

"Daphne."

Her eyes landed on me, not a hint of life sparking behind them.

"I don't want to hear anything you have to say, Cain. You've hurt me in every possible way and I'm done with you, too."

Her words, the look on her face, all of it was a kick to the balls.

She was hurt and broken. And I'd been the one to break her.

"Please, Daph. Everything I said to you last night... I didn't mean it."

I closed the space between us, but she turned her head, refusing to look at me.

"I was stupid and selfish and I was lying to myself. I thought if I ignored everything between us and acted like I didn't care, it would make it true." I reached for her hand, but she pulled away. "Our parents saw a video of us together that night at your house."

Her eyes snapped to mine, then she glanced at both her parents.

"Your father showed it to my father and he threatened to take away everything. My tuition, my spot on the team, and my shot at the NBA."

Her brow pinched, the first sign the real Daphne was still in there.

"I was weak and selfish and I chose my own future over a future with you. But I don't want it. None of it means anything without you."

Her eyes filled with tears she was clearly trying to fight.

"You told me you wanted me, that you were choosing me, and I told you I didn't feel the same way." I shook my head, never taking my eyes off her. "It was the biggest fucking lie I've ever told."

I reached for her hand and this time she didn't pull away.

She stared down at it, then back at me. "I don't trust you."

I nodded. "I know. So, let's start again. No more lies, no more games. Just you and me."

She stared up at me, searching for something in my expression.

Then her eyes softened, sparking with a hint of life.

"Okay."

I frowned. "Okay?"

She nodded. "Okay. But only because I love you."

I tugged her to my chest, wrapping my arms around her. She buried her face against my shirt.

I kissed the top of her head. "I'm so sorry, Daph."

She lifted her head and I dropped my forehead to hers.

"I fucking love you."

She gave me a small smile. "I love you, too."

We glanced up, all eyes in the room on us, and I held Daphne tighter to my side.

"This is not happening...." Mr Montaigne started, advancing on us like he was going to tear Daphne away from me if that's what it took.

"Enough!"

Everyone stilled. Only it wasn't my father who'd spoken.

It was my mother, red-faced with disbelief.

"I'm appalled at the things I've heard tonight. I won't let any of you force two of our children into a marriage neither of them wants to further our own interests. That marriage would clearly destroy all three of them."

She glanced at me, then at Daphne.

"Cain and Daphne have been in love with each other

since they were children. You'd have to be blind and stupid not to see it."

She turned on my father.

"I sat by and let you nudge Kyle and Daphne together to suit your business. But somewhere along the line, this nudging has turned into something far more serious. Daphne is right. We shouldn't be using our own children like pawns in a game they're not even playing. If your business relationships aren't strong enough based on the decades of friendship between our two families, then find people more worthy of doing business with."

She shook her head.

"Daphne and Cain love each other and no one is going to stand in the way of that anymore."

Kyle scowled. "Don't I get a say in all of this? Daphne is my girlfriend."

I tensed, grinding my teeth. "You never cared about Daphne. You only cared about how much dating her made Daddy love you."

My father's gaze narrowed. "Some sons like to make their fathers proud."

I huffed a humorless laugh. "You don't want me to make you proud. You want me to live my life the way you dictate and I'm not interested. But don't worry, Dad, Kyle will be there to take over when you eventually retire."

Mr Montaigne growled in frustration. "I've had enough of this." He turned to my mother. "I'm sorry, Vivian, but I don't agree to this."

"There's nothing you can do about it," came Daphne's quiet voice.

She pushed from my arms, coming to stand in front of me and I stepped closer, my chest at her back.

"Like hell there isn't," Mr Montaigne said. "Where do

you plan on getting the money for college when I cut you off?"

"From me."

Mr Montaigne spun around to stare daggers at my mother, but didn't dare utter a word against her. Not when there was so much money at stake between our two families.

He rounded on his wife instead. "You support this?"

Mrs Montaigne glanced at her daughter, mouth opening and closing again. Then stared at me.

"This was never about you, Cain. It was business. You understand that?"

I didn't respond, because it didn't matter anymore. Daphne was done with Kyle. What our parents wanted no longer mattered.

Mrs Montaigne turned back to her husband. "Let's go. This is done."

"You can't be serious!" Kyle said, eyes blazing. "Daphne is mine!"

I rolled my eyes and Daphne rounded on him.

"I'm not some prize you can claim. I'm a real person, Kyle, with feelings and needs. I get to choose who I want to be with." She leaned back against me, her head fitting under my chin. "I want to be with Cain."

"Dad, come on..." Kyle appealed to our father.

My father's jaw ticked. He hated to lose and this was the ultimate loss.

"It's done, Kyle. It's over."

Kyle's face reddened so fast he looked like he might combust and he stormed out. "Screw all of you!"

"Dad?" Daphne said, staring at her father, hope in her voice.

He stared back, his expression tight with anger. "I know

when I'm overruled, but I'm not going to pretend to be happy about it." He eyed me with contempt, then turned to his wife. "Let's go."

He marched to the door and Daphne deflated at his dismissal. I wrapped my arms around her from behind, running my nose along the sensitive skin behind her ear and relishing the small shiver that ran down her spine.

Mrs Montaigne shared a look with my mother before giving us a tight smile. "He'll come around." Then she followed him out the door.

"Well," my mother said, smiling broadly at the both of us. "What now?"

Epilogue

DAPHNE

I bounced from foot to foot, cracking my neck and shaking out all my nervous energy.

One more point and I'd win not only my match, but Stanford the NCAA D1 women's tournament.

No pressure.

Stepping up to the service line, I bounced the ball twice, glancing at the other end of the court before tossing the ball in the air and swinging my racquet hard.

The ball sliced perfectly as it connected with my racquet and sailed across the net to my opponent. She sent it back a few feet to my left and I shuffled there, hitting it straight back at her.

She had to dive for it this time, just getting her racquet to it in time to get it back over the net. But the hit was weak, the shot placement terrible, so I lined it up, putting all my power into my backhand to send it flying. My opponent was too slow this time, the ball hitting the ground just inside the line.

I gripped my racquet and screamed up at the sky in victory, my teammates rushing me from the sideline and wrapping me up in a hug.

"We did it! We actually freaking did it!" my teammate Bea shouted, tears in her eyes.

Cain was on his feet in the crowd, along with the two of his UCLA teammates who had made the trip with him. They'd cheered me on the whole match, making the crowd laugh with their shouts into the silence ahead of my serve once or twice.

I pushed free from my teammates and ran to where Cain was sitting. I stepped up on the bench, pulling myself up and Cain leaned over the barricade, taking my face in his hands and kissing me.

"You killed it, Daph. I knew you would."

I smiled. "I'm glad one of us did."

"I've always believed in you, babe. Since you were six and only just learning to hold a racquet."

My heart swelled at his words. "Thank you for coming to support me. I know it's a long drive."

It was a six-hour one-way trip from UCLA and he and his teammates had to ask special permission from his coach. But he'd come out to watch me play four times already this year, after I'd made the Stanford tournament team as a freshman.

"I don't care about the drive. There's nowhere I'd rather be."

I grinned up at him. "You going to help me celebrate later, then?"

"You fucking know it."

***

Cain shoved me against the back of his hotel room door, crowding me with his hard body.

"Those workouts at UCLA are really paying off, super-star," I said between desperate breaths, Cain's mouth connecting with my throat.

"You think so?" he murmured against my skin, nipping at me with his teeth, his warm, wet tongue following behind to soothe the sting.

The sensation made my core clench with need.

We hadn't seen each other in two months. Cain's game schedule was more hectic than usual while I was busy training for the tournament with my team.

We tried to visit each other as much as we could. We talked on the phone every day, but it wasn't the same as the feel of him pressed against me and his mouth on my skin.

Or him buried deep inside me.

"I've missed you so fucking much, Daph..."

He pulled back from my throat, mouth closing over mine and tongue diving into my mouth.

I kissed him back, clawing at his back to bring him closer.

Stripping off my shirt, he kissed over my collarbones and down my stomach. His hands ducked under my skirt, sliding my panties down my legs.

"These lace thongs drive me wild. I think about the way your ass looks in them when I beat off to images of you. Remember last time when you let me fuck you in my car just like our first time?"

"Yes," I said, sucking in a breath when his finger slid inside me.

"Jesus, Daph, you're ready to go."

I gave him a lust-fueled smile. "That's what you do to me. All I have to do is look at you and I'm ready."

Cain smirked, dropping to his knees and shoving my skirt up to my hips.

"Fuck, I've missed this."

I didn't have time to respond before he dove between my legs, tongue sliding over me and making me moan.

Cain sucked and licked and teased me until I was teetering on the edge.

"I don't want to come without you inside me," I breathed, trying to fight the pleasure threatening to take hold.

Without a word, Cain scooped my legs out from under me and threw me on the bed. Then yanked his shirt over his head, showing off his perfectly chiseled chest.

"My favorite sight," I said with a sigh.

He dropped his pants, his enormous erection springing free.

"Okay, my second favorite sight. That's my favorite sight."

I bit my lip as my mind flooded with all the things he'd done to me in the past, and would do to me again now that we had all night.

Cain took hold of his hard length, stroking it up and down a few times. "Don't look at me like that."

"Like what?"

"Like you want to suck me dry."

"I do," I said, pushing up on my elbows.

"No time. I need to be buried deep inside you. Now."

He dragged the tip of his cock over my slick folds, teasing me.

"Cain," I breathed, falling back on the bed as pleasure rippled through me.

"Yeah, baby?"

I lifted my head, biting my bottom lip. "Fuck me already."

The left side of his perfect mouth pulled up in a smirk.

"Be careful what you wish for, baby."

Then he slammed into me, making me moan.

THE END

If you enjoyed *HATED YOU FIRST*, I'd love it if you would take a second to leave a quick review!

And read on for a sneak peek at chapter one of book two - *LOVED YOU FIRST* - Kyle's story after the events of *HATED YOU FIRST*.

Also by Elouise Tynan

BULLY ROMANCE

HATED YOU FIRST / LOVED YOU FIRST NOVELLA DUOLOGY

BOOK TWO - LOVED YOU FIRST - FROM KYLE'S POINT OF VIEW
COMING 2023

COLLEGE SPORTS ROMANCE

PIERSON U SERIES

WAITING TO SCORE

A fake dating college sports romance

READ NOW

SHOOTING TO WIN

A forced proximity second chance romance

READ NOW

** BANT + IMOGEN'S BOOK - COMING 2023 **

Acknowledgments

Thank you for reading this story!

I'm so lucky to have the readers I do and I don't take a single one of you for granted for a minute.

This is my first foray into the world of bully romance (longtime reader, first-time writer in the genre) so I want to give special thanks to Sam (@samreadsromance), Jess (@fromthebookshelfofdreams), Hillary (@bookishhill) and Jordan (@jlreadss), who answered my call on Instagram to read this for me when I was questioning if Cain was mean enough to Daphne for this to be a true bully romance! Your insights were so valuable and I appreciate you so much. You are bookish angels of the highest order.

Thank you, as always, to my amazing critique partners, Steph and Mel, who read anything I send them without hesitation and give me the world's best feedback to help make these stories great.

Thank you to Mel at Write On Editorial for her edits and Quirah at Temptation Creations for the cover.

And thank *YOU* again for reading this.

You're my favourite.

Keep reading for a sneak peek at book two - *LOVED YOU FIRST* - from Kyle's point of view.

About the Author

Elouise Tynan is a romance author obsessed with kissing stories about strong heroines and swoony heroes mixed with laughter, a whole lot of love and a little bit of heat.

She lives in Melbourne, Australia with her husband and son.

Connect with Elouise and come chat all things books:

Instagram: @elouisetynanwrites
TikTok: @elouisetynanwrites

EXCERPT: CHAPTER ONE

LOVED YOU FIRST (BOOK 2)

Kyle Cashman's spicy bully romance novella

KYLE

"I'm so into you," the girl riding me said between pants, bouncing her naked B-cups in my face.

I gave her a grunt in response, gripping her hips tighter and bouncing her a little harder on my lap.

"This is more than casual hooking up for me. It is for you too, right?" she asked.

Fuck, no.

It had been an epic mistake sleeping with her more than twice. A mistake I never usually made. Give a girl enough world-altering orgasms and she was ready for matrimony and matching Range Rovers.

Since getting to college, I'd made a point of never railing

the same girl more than twice. Three rides and they were hooked.

But Prue was fucking hot. And when she'd snaked her smoking body around mine at the party raging on the other side of the door when I was already five drinks deep, moaning in my ear about how desperate she was to have my cock in her mouth, my better judgment had gone out the window faster than I could jerk it to memories of my ex-girlfriend bent over my backseat.

Fucking Daphne.

She'd fucked me over and was now fucking my brother instead.

I scowled at the memory.

I'd spent my entire first semester at Harvard trying to bang her from my mind with any hot girl who was willing.

"Kyle?" Prue frowned down at me, still riding me hard. "I mean something to you, right?"

I held back my eye roll.

"Yeah, baby. You mean something to me."

I slammed her down on my dick, making her cry out and getting me a step closer to coming. I focused my efforts, pounding into her with enough force she was likely to hit the ceiling.

"Oh my God, Kyle," Prue moaned, loving every second.

Her nails dug into my shoulders, the bite of pain pushing me closer to the edge.

We came at the same time, pleasure shooting through me straight to my dick.

Prue smiled down at me, sweaty and satiated, trying to wrap her arms around my neck to snuggle against me.

Fuck that. I don't fucking snuggle.

Not anymore.

I wrapped an arm around her waist, lifting her from my

lap and sliding her onto the sofa beside me. Then I tucked my dick back in my jeans and zipped up, getting to my feet.

"Kyle, what the hell..." Prue protested, fingers locking around my wrist. "You said I meant something to you."

I looked down at her, her cheeks flushed from being freshly fucked.

"You do mean something to me. You're a hole I had a good time filling and now it's done."

Hurt flashed across her face, before it pinched in a scowl, but I ignored her, pulling my hand free and striding for the door.

"You're an asshole, you know that?" Prue called after me. "Whoever fucking broke you did one hell of a job."

Her words hit me like a blow to the chest, but I immediately shut it down, reaching for a shot from a passing tray as I re-joined the party.

I'd had an entire future planned out before Daphne had ripped my fucking heart out by riding my brother. But I'd rather toss my dick in a blender than ever admit that to anyone.

My ex-girlfriend was gone, I had to stop being such a little bitch about it.

There was plenty more pussy at college.

And I was determined to sample all of it.

BOOK 2 COMING IN 2023

Visit www.elouisetynan.com to sign up to my newsletter to be the first to know!

EXCERPT: CHAPTER ONE

WAITING TO SCORE (PIERSON U BOOK 1)

A fake dating college sports romance

———

MONTY

I slid my hand into his before I knew what I was doing.

His palm was warm and solid and unexpectedly large.

I dared a glance over my shoulder searching for that mop of dirty blond hair I didn't want to see coming through the crowd.

"Can I help you?" the guy beside me asked, glancing down at our joined hands, then at me.

I turned to face him, my eyebrows shooting up my forehead.

He was *stupidly* hot. Straight nose, light brown hair, and striking blue eyes surrounded by dark lashes that would be the envy of any woman. And that jaw. That jaw put sharp-cut diamonds to shame.

"I... um...."

I was suddenly finding it hard to remember why I was holding hands with a guy who looked like he'd stepped off the set of *Riverdale*.

"Oh, I can't wait to hear this," one of Hot Guy's friends said, his eyes shining with humor. All three of them waited, clearly expecting an explanation for why I'd attached myself to a random guy on the quad. In my defense, I didn't know he was so damn hot. His hand had been the closest in my time of need, so I'd taken it.

Hot Guy tried to pull away just as the very face I didn't want to see appeared through the crowd of students gathered on the quad.

"Wait!" I gripped his arm to stop him. "Pretend to be my boyfriend. I'll pay you."

He looked at me like I'd just offered to blow him with a mouthful of herpes. Which to be fair, I could kind of understand. Not because I had mouth herpes. But who grabbed a total stranger and begged them to play pretend couple? As far as first impressions went, this one was insane.

"I don't need your money," he said, frowning down at me.

Holy shit, he was tall. Had he been this tall ten seconds ago or was it just the irritation starting to cloud his face that made him more imposing?

"Please? Just do me this favor and I'll give you whatever you want." I gave him what I hoped was my most pleading and innocent smile.

"Oh, this just keeps getting better and better," his friend said, both his buddies trying and failing to hold in their laughter.

A glance in my periphery showed that mop of dirty blond hair closing in.

"Are you for real right now?" Hot Guy asked, eyes darting around the quad. "Do we know each other? Did Davis put you up to this?"

He ran his free hand—the one not currently taken hostage by me—through his hair, the muscles of his bicep flexing to show off a seriously toned arm.

My gaze snagged on his clothes, eyes running over him and his two friends. They were all dressed the same—Nike sneakers, navy sweat shorts and a navy Pierson University basketball t-shirt.

Basketball players, damn it. Didn't this just kept getting better and better?

I'd thoroughly humiliated myself in front of some of the most wanted guys on campus. I'd have to make time to be embarrassed later. Right now, I was desperate. And I was out of time.

"This isn't a joke. I swear I'm not crazy, I just need your help."

Hot Guy's eyes roamed my face, taking up seconds I didn't have, which meant I was about to do something that would solidify me as the most bat-shit girl these guys had ever accidentally encountered.

"I'm so sorry in advance for this."

A question formed in Hot Guy's eyes, but he didn't get a chance to ask it because I gripped his face, tugging his mouth to mine. Kissing him was like kissing a stone wall of surprise, and I screwed my eyes shut, heat flooding my cheeks at my own ridiculousness.

Desperate times and all that... but it still didn't change the fact I'd jumped a perfect stranger. An incredibly *hot* stranger.

I slid my fingers through his hair and his mouth relaxed against mine, his surprise morphing into something much friendlier. His hand closed over my hip, making me squeak, his other hand sliding over my ass. My lips parted all on their own, his tongue sweeping into my mouth in lazy, practiced strokes.

God, he was a good kisser.

Scratch that, he was a phenomenal kisser. And if this kiss went on for the rest of the week, I'd die hot and happy.

"Well, that escalated quickly," one of his friends said, but I barely heard him, too wrapped up in Hot Guy's hands on my body and his tongue in my mouth.

That was, until I heard the one voice that was like a bucket of ice water down my back.

"Monty?"

I stiffened, turning my head, lips still attached to Hot Guy and his fingers still curled around my hips.

Plastering a look of surprise on my face, I reluctantly pulled my mouth away, and I could have sworn Hot Guy frowned in annoyance.

"Alec."

My dirty-blond ex-boyfriend looked me up and down, blowing out a breath. "I thought it was you. I knew you'd transferred to Pierson. I was hoping to run into you."

I turned in Hot Guy's hold so my back was to his chest, pulling his muscular arms around my waist, hoping it looked like he was holding onto me willingly.

"Well, here I am!" I said to Alec a little too brightly.

No need to overcompensate just because I'd found myself in the most awkward situation of my entire life. One of my own ridiculous making.

I hesitated for the briefest moment over the words I was about to utter. But I'd come this far. Time to shoot my shot and pray to everything that was holy Hot Guy would play along.

"I transferred here a few weeks ago to be closer to my boyfriend." I slapped a hand over Hot Guy's at my waist and smiled at him over my shoulder.

Those intense blue eyes stared down at me, making my heart pound in my chest.

Please don't out me. Please don't out me. Please don't out me.

His gaze slid to Alec, and he extended his hand. "Nice to meet you, bro. I'm West."

West. He even had a hot guy name.

Alec stared at West's offered hand then ignored it completely, his gaze cutting back to me.

"Since when do you have a boyfriend? I spoke to your mom last week, and she didn't mention it."

Shit. He had me there. Anyone who knew me at all knew I told my mom everything. Well, *almost* everything. I hadn't told her about the way Alec had been acting this past year.

"No, well..." I said, fumbling for an explanation. "We've been keeping this pretty quiet. Just between us, you know?"

Alec's gaze narrowed. "Why?"

God, his persistence was annoying. Why did he even care?

I worked to think of a lie, my mind offering up a sum total of nothing.

"Oh, um...." I bit the inside of my cheek.

West's arms tightened around my waist. "Because I'm on the basketball team."

He bent over, resting his chin on my shoulder and his cheek against mine as if he'd done it a thousand times before. I sagged against him in relief, the smell of his cologne invading my senses. He smelled incredible, had a face Taylor Swift would write songs about, and he was helping me lie to Alec. I'd really lucked out with my choice of fake boyfriend.

"So?" Alec asked, gaze finally cutting to West to size him up.

West stood tall, hands sliding off my waist to sling an arm around my shoulders and tuck me to his side. I fit perfectly beneath his arm, the two of us at just the right heights.

"The female fans can be a little crazy, man," West's buddy offered, and I shot him a grateful smile.

So grateful I could cry. They had no idea what they were saving me from.

"He's not kidding," the other friend added. "I once came home to find a naked basketball bunny in my bed inside my *locked* dorm room." He shuddered.

"I mean... you didn't have to let her blow you, dude. You could have kicked her out," the first one said, the corners of his mouth twitching.

The second one shrugged, clearly perplexed at the suggestion of turning away a naked girl, even if she wasn't opposed to a little breaking and entering.

"I didn't want to subject Monty to all that, at least not right away," West said as though it were nothing and not some of the sweetest, most considerate words a college guy had probably ever uttered in defense of the random girl he'd met three minutes ago.

I tilted my head up at him with what I hoped was a look of pure adoration. It wasn't that much of a stretch at this point, given he and his friends were officially my campus knights.

"We wanted to take the time to make sure this was

right before we went public and told our families." West's intense blue eyes stared down at me, his hand coming up to stroke my cheek, the touch sending a shiver skittering over my skin. "But we know that it's right. I couldn't be more into this girl."

My stomach swooped, my lusty lady parts clearly not getting the memo that we were faking it.

Alec cleared his throat, and I reluctantly pulled my gaze from West's.

"There are things we need to talk about," Alec said, back to ignoring my fake boyfriend completely. "Can we have dinner one night this week?"

I opened my mouth to reply, mind scrolling through all the ways I could rebuff that idea without encouraging Alec any further than I somehow already had, when West cut in.

"Oh yeah, man, of course. We'd love to have dinner. Name a time and place and we'll be there. I recommend Ruby's. They do one hell of a burger."

He offered Alec a killer smile, all straight white teeth and shining blue eyes, and I bit my lip to stifle my laugh.

"Sure, whatever," Alec said tightly, his eyes never leaving me. "I'll text you, Monty."

Please don't, I thought as Alec turned to go.

"Nice to meet you, bro. Looking forward to that catch up," West called.

Alec slipped through the crowd on the quad, throwing a look over his shoulder.

West smiled broadly, raising a hand to wave, but I grabbed his wrist, pulling it down and swinging out from under him.

He raised an eyebrow at me in question.

"So, about that..." I said, heat creeping into my cheeks.

"Girl, that was some of the best shit I've seen all week!" West's friend said, throwing his head back with a laugh.

"Did you clock West's face when she kissed him?" the other asked.

West's glare shut them both up.

"Friend of yours?" he asked me.

"Ex."

"I figured. Care to give me a little more info about why you just sucked my face off in front of him?"

I screwed up my face. "Excuse me, that kiss was some of my best work. It's not my fault kissing you was like making out with one of the marble statues outside the library."

His eyebrows shot up.

"Oh, she didn't," West's teammate said, bending over to press his hands to his knees.

"She did," the other one said, looking awed. "She just compared the King of Campus to a stone statue."

West's jaw clenched. "Don't you two have somewhere else to be?"

"We don't, actually."

"Find somewhere," West said.

Shooting me broad grins, they strolled away, not bothering to cover their laughter, which filtered back to us through the busy quad.

I crossed my arms over my chest. "King of Campus, huh? That's quite a title."

He shrugged. "It's the basketball jersey they want."

"Are you the captain?"

"Hell no."

"Just the team stud?"

"Yeah. I mean, no." He looked momentarily flustered, and I tried not to laugh. "This isn't about me."

"Maybe it should be," I said as my phone buzzed in my

pocket. I pulled it out to read a text from my friend Stella, speaking absently to West. "Your story sounds a hell of a lot more interesting than mine."

He crossed his impressive arms over his even more impressive chest, those blue eyes scanning me and making my stomach twist in the best way. "I'd rather hear yours."

"And it's a story I'd love to tell you," I said, shoving my phone back in the pocket of my denim cut-offs. "But I have to go."

"Are you serious?"

I screwed up my nose and pointed at my pocket. "Emergency SOS text, I'm needed elsewhere." I backed away, edging around a nearby group of students. "But thank you. You really helped me out of a jam. You're a prince and a gentleman and all those other great things men hope to be."

"Monty..."

The sound of my name coming from his mouth was something else.

"I'm sorry!" I called. "I absolutely owe you one!"

He shook his head in disbelief, and I jogged down the path, thanking the college Gods for delivering me such a perfect boy to accost in my time of need.

Maybe this new school was going to be fun after all.

Want to keep reading?
Get *WAITING TO SCORE*

(available in ebook, paperback
or discreet cover paperback)

www.ingramcontent.com/pod-product-compliance
Lightning Source LLC
Chambersburg PA
CBHW071929130726
47909CB00014B/2699